Helda had lost her f
she was losing Ran

His expression was so f
him if he would keep in t
"You've been so good to me, Rance, and Dad thought of
you very highly. If. . .if there's ever anything I can do to
help you, will you let me know?" she finished in a rush as
she saw him start to scowl.

"I'm not sure if that would be wise, Hildie," he said
very softly after a brief pause. He straightened and added
decisively, "I'd better go, or I'll be keeping the Stevenses
out of bed too late."

Rance strode outside, and Hildie trailed miserably after
him, wondering what he meant. At the top of the steps,
he turned. When she reached him, they stared at each
other silently. Then she saw him swallow convulsively.
As though he could not help himself, he reached out his
hand and slid a gentle finger down her soft cheek, leaving a trail of fire that ignited Hilda's senses.

As she drew in a sharp breath, he said very quietly,
"Don't come down to the car with me."

She stood frozen, frantically trying to think of something to say that would stop him leaving like this.

He whispered, "Bye, Hildie love," and turned and disappeared into the blackness of the night.

MARY HAWKINS lives in Austrailia with her husband; they have three grown children. Her first inspirational novel, *Search for Tomorrow*, was voted the second most favorite contemporary by **Heartsong Presents** readers.

Books by Mary Hawkins

HEARTSONG PRESENTS
HP42—Search for Tomorrow
HP101—Damaged Dreams

Search
for Yesterday

Mary Hawkins

A sequel to *Search for Tomorrow*

Heartsong Presents

To my delightful daughter, Gaylene, who has helped so much in the plotting and dreaming of my stories. Also in memory of our own beautiful Trixie— the Polly of this story— who died during the writing of this book.

A note from the Author:
I love to hear from my readers! You may write to me at the following address: **Mary Hawkins**
                                      Author Relations
                                      P.O. Box 719
                                      Uhrichsville, OH 44683

ISBN 1-55748-707-3

SEARCH FOR YESTERDAY

Cover illustration by Kay Salem.

one

". . .And that's when I pronounce you man and wife. Then you can lift the veil back and kiss Gail." The Reverend Rance Telford's deep tones were very matter of fact.

Hilda shivered. She heard Jim Stevens ask a question with laughter in his voice. Then he bent over and kissed Gail Brandon's flushed, smiling face.

Looking away from the group at the front of the small church, Hilda clenched her hands tightly. She swallowed painfully, forcing the tears back.

Why on earth didn't I suggest they pick up Dad for this rotten rehearsal? she thought despairingly, and then looked over at the slight, grey-haired man at the organ. *Because you knew he wouldn't be able to get home with them until much later, and he's really still not very well.*

But deep down, Hilda knew that was only part of her reason. She did want her father to be back home as soon as possible, but she had bitterly been forced to acknowledge the real reason to herself. She was too proud to let Jim and Gail think their wedding rehearsal would be so painful she couldn't be here. And she still had to survive the wedding itself anyway.

Jean Drew's soft voice made her give a little jump. "Are they nearly finished, Hilda?"

She glanced up at the older woman who had come to stand in the back aisle behind her. "I'm. . .I'm not sure," she said jerkily.

As she looked down at her, Jean's eyes narrowed. "Are

5

you all right, Hilda?"

Hilda suddenly realized she had not managed to stop all the tears. Hurriedly she brushed at her cheeks with the back of a hand. "Just. . .just feeling a bit nostalgic I suppose. I grew up with Beth and. . .and Jim."

Her husky words sounded forlorn, defensive, even to her own ears. She felt a blush creeping into her face, and quickly looked away.

"Yes, I know. You joined us on several outings the times I've managed to visit over the years."

Jean's quiet voice was full of compassion, and Hilda gritted her teeth. Of course Jim's mother's best friend from Sydney would know what an absolute fool she had made of herself over Jim last year.

"Are you sure you wouldn't like to help Marian and me with the flowers for the service?"

Hilda tensed.

Jean must have noticed her reaction and added swiftly, "I mean for tomorrow morning. Marian and I decided we just had to put at least one bowl of red roses in here for Good Friday even if they don't last until the wedding Saturday morning. But somehow that one bowl has grown." Her voice filled with amusement at her old friend who was making her way through the pews to join them. "The mother of the bridegroom is getting a bit carried away out there!"

"Oh, is she just!"

Hilda closed her eyes briefly, and then turned and managed a smile up at Marian Stevens. Pain lashed her as she saw the laughter in the familiar faded blue eyes disappear once they looked at her.

"It was good of you to drive Bob here, Hilda," Marian said briefly.

"He's still not really over the flu," Hilda responded

sharply, looking back at her father. "He shouldn't even be out in the cool night air."

Her father must have heard her raised voice and glanced across at her. He looked anxious for a moment, and then smiled gently. She loved him dearly and even more these past long months for his wonderful support since Jim had told her he and Gail Brandon were going to be married. She forced an answering smile, and saw his smile widen and his lined face relax with relief.

Hilda thought she had come to grips with the fact that the dream she had nurtured for years of one day being Jim's wife was dead. But now pain knifed through her again as she looked back at the bridal party. Gail's attendants were Ann Green, one of her nursing friends from Sydney, and Jim's younger sister, Beth.

Beth was the same age as Hilda, and so they had always been in the same class right through school. An only child of older parents, Hilda had often been lonely and had loved spending as much time as she could wangle at the neighbours farm a few kilometres away across the flat black soil paddocks.

Through the years Jim had been like a brother. Then, within a few years, Hilda's mother had died and Beth had left home when she had married Arthur Smith. Hilda and Jim had been left a twosome, and as always, continued sharing transport to parties and outings in the farming community. But that had all begun to change early last year.

And then Gail had arrived.

There was a combined burst of laughter from the bridal party, and Rance Telford began ushering Jim and Gail toward the tiny vestry behind the platform.

"About time," said Jean with a relieved sigh. She turned and followed Marian back quickly to the kitchen to start bringing out the flowers.

"Well, that's all they need me for. We can go when you're ready, love."

Hilda started at her father's voice. She had been watching Jim's tall, dark figure towering over the slighter, fairer minister. She turned her head quickly, and then caught her breath.

"Dad, you look dreadful!" she exclaimed. "I wish you'd let them get someone else to play the organ, especially tomorrow, even if you do the wedding on Saturday."

Bob Garrett ran a hand over his weathered, lined face. "I am rather tired. That bout of flu certainly did a good job on me," he sighed and then shook his head. "But I'm feeling stronger every day, and I'll be fine. Besides, the only other musician is away for the weekend."

Hilda studied the pallor of his face doubtfully. He hated being fussed over, especially since her mother had died, so she bit her lip instead of protesting further.

"You did check with Mr. Telford about staying with us tonight, didn't you?" she murmured as she stood up.

"Botheration! I forgot all about it!" Mr Garrett hesitated, and then sighed heavily as he turned back.

"You go on out to the car, Dad. I'll ask him," Hilda said hurriedly, and then her heart sank. It would mean intruding on the group in the vestry.

Reluctantly, she knocked gently on the vestry door before opening it. Faces were turned toward her, and hurt slashed her as the radiant smiles on Jim and Gail's faces were replaced by wariness.

"Dad...Dad forgot to ask Mr. Telford if he had decided to stay with us instead of driving all the way back to Toowoomba tonight," she blurted out hurriedly, avoiding their eyes and looking at the minister.

"Oh, Hildie, I'm sorry. I meant to ring you." Rance Telford stood as he put up a hand to push back his already ruffled light brown hair. "Yes, please. I'd love to stay tonight, and tomorrow too if I could." He walked across to her, and then looked anxious. "Are you sure it won't be too much trouble, especially since your father's been sick?"

"Oh, no," she said hastily, "he's really hoping you can come."

A rather wry look crossed the handsome face looking down at her. Heat rose to her own face.

"And. . .and I have too, of course. I. . .I mean. . .we've been looking forward to. . .to having you stay," she stammered awkwardly, and not quite truthfully. The last thing she had felt like this dreadful Easter weekend was having a guest stay. Especially the minister!

A slightly rueful grin tilted Rance's well-shaped lips. She felt the colour flooding her face even more. He knew.

"I. . .I wondered if you'd like to go for a picnic after church tomorrow. To the Bunya Mountains perhaps?" she added impulsively, and tilted her chin as surprise filled his face.

"Why, what a lovely idea," Gail Brandon exclaimed. "Jim took us there a few weeks ago."

A sharp pang shot through Hilda. She deliberately kept her eyes on Rance Telford's face, hoping he had not noticed her reaction. Once she would have automatically accompanied the Stevens on an outing like that.

The amber eyes staring down at her were piercing all of a sudden. "We'll see how we go tomorrow, perhaps," Rance said briefly.

Somehow Hilda managed to smile broadly at the young couple. "Best wishes on Saturday, you two. I'd better get Dad home now."

As she started to turn away, she glanced at Rance Telford. All the way home, the look of surprised approval that she had seen in his eyes somehow comforted her, as at the same time it embarrassed her. So even their minister was aware of the rumours she had deliberately fostered last year about her relationship with Jim.

About fifteen minutes later, lost in thought, she stopped the car to let her father out before continuing to the garage.

She did not realize how quiet she had been until instead of opening his door, he reached across and patted her gently on her hand. "It will get easier, sweetheart. Just give it more time."

"Oh, Dad," she said miserably. "Everybody knows, even Rance Telford."

"No, I don't agree. Jim and Marian would never have said anything to hurt you deliberately. And since Gail made a personal commitment to Christ, she has lost all her old bitterness and anger. None of them would want to hurt you."

She stiffened. "Wouldn't they?" Her voice was harsh.

He sighed wearily. "I think you should know them well enough to know that, Hildie." There was quiet reproof in his voice, and she refrained from answering him as he opened his door. "I won't wait up for Rance. He'll be a while yet and you can look after him. Goodnight," he said briefly.

She watched him walk slowly across the rough gravel, lit by the headlights, until he stepped onto the area of lawn the outside light reached. As she watched his slight, stooped shoulders, bitter regret lashed her. Perhaps it would have been better if she had not blurted it all out to him last year when Jim and Gail had announced their engagement. He was hurting for her, and she loved him for it, but she doubted if he could really understand the depth of her own hurt and humiliation.

She had never really thought about her father's age. Now it hit her that he would soon be seventy. He was really an old man. As long as she could remember his hair had been grey, but now it was much whiter.

When her mother had died, something seemed to have died in him also. Although he was still the gentle, loving man he had always been, he had never really regained his old exuberance and drive. And this bout of illness had taken such a lot out of him.

She garaged the car in the large shed a short distance from the house. As she strolled back to the house, weariness dragged her feet. Suddenly she wished she could just curl up on her bed, wake up in the morning to find the wedding was all over, and somehow discover her heart had stopped aching. But sleep had only come easily lately when she had been totally exhausted. And that had been most nights since her father had been sick.

With a sigh she sank onto the cane lounge on that part of the verandah only faintly lit and stared out across the yard where the outdoor light had changed the garden to a mysterious place of softly swaying shadows. There was a movement beside her, and a soft, moist nose nudged her arm.

"So there you are, Polly," she murmured to the brown and white collie, as she turned to fondle her. "And how are you tonight, mmmh? Too lazy to greet us at the car?"

The dog whimpered softly, and sat beside her. One paw came up to rest on her lap. Hilda stopped rubbing the spot behind the drooping ears, and lifted the long nose to examine it in the faint light. "And are you still dribbling that rotten pink stuff from your nose, I wonder?"

Another reason to be worried. Polly had developed a slight lump on the nose, just between her eyes. And just that morning Hilda had noticed a discharge had started.

Hilda sighed. "Well, it's probably only a cyst of some sort, but it's to the vet for you. Right after Easter."

The dog settled down beside her feet, and Hilda felt a little comforted as she relaxed, her gaze returning to the shadows.

It was the crunch of gravel under swift strides that brought her awake. As she stirred and sat up a little stiffly, Polly rose and ambled over toward the steps. The man stopped with one foot on the bottom step.

"Hi, Polly. Not going to eat me tonight?" Rance Telford's deep voice murmured.

The dog's tail moved enthusiastically from side to side and she bounded down the steps. Then, to Hilda's astonishment, she opened her mouth and "talked" to him as only a collie could. When Polly had been a small puppy they had tried to train her not to bark when they arrived home, and she had ever since greeted them by what a very young Hilda had called "Collie lingo."

"Well! I've never heard her do that to anyone except Dad and me. . .and Mum," Hilda exclaimed as she stood up. "Not even Jim—" She broke off, biting her lip.

Rance paused in stroking the dog and peered toward her as she moved out from the shadows of the verandah. "We've become good friends since I've spent so much time with your father these past weeks." He studied her face. "I've kept you up," he said regretfully and joined her on the verandah. "You look very tired."

"I was out on the tractor at dawn," Hilda said abruptly, self-consciously tucking a strand of her dark copper hair behind one ear. "With Dad being sick, it's a battle to get the sorghum stubble ploughed in and the other paddocks ready for the wheat planting."

He stood stock still. "I knew you'd been working on the tractor, but you haven't been doing all the work by yourself, have you?"

"And why not," she snapped, feeling suddenly defensive. "I've always helped where I could on the farm, including driving the tractor when Dad would let me. And since he's been sick there's been no choice. The ground has to be ploughed and fertilized, ready for planting at the end of May or beginning of June. As soon as it rains. It might be between seasons and the sorghum harvest finished, but it's still a busy time. And with Dad being sick there's still a lot to do. I've got to finish before the forecast storms come and make the black soil bog down any foolish vehicle daring to venture onto it."

"But wasn't there anyone you could employ? I'm sure someone from church would have helped."

Hilda tilted her chin and glared at him, not for a moment prepared to admit she had gone very much against Bob Garrett's wishes by taking over the tractor completely, working from sunrise to sunset.

"Any men who've helped out in the past are already working flat out," she said defiantly. "The cotton farmers on the Downs are in the middle of their harvest now." Then she paused, and for some inexplicable reason she found a grin twitching her lips at his horrified face. "We farm girls are tough, you know. Not like your city-slicker ones."

An answering smile touched his face. "Not so much of the 'my' city slickers, thank you. I was reared on a farm, too. Admittedly it was a dairy farm closer to Toowoomba and a much smaller acreage than the farms out here." The smile disappeared. "But Mum certainly never had to drive the tractor, and I had no sisters." The expression on his face changed again. He hesitated for a moment, and then tilted his chin and added steadily, "I thought you of all people would have learnt not to underestimate girls from the city, Hildie."

All amusement was wiped out of Hilda at his sharp response. She fought for control as she stared at him. So even their minister condemned her.

"Did. . .did Dad tell you. . .?" Her throat seized up.

"No. Except to ask me to pray for you because you were going through a rough time," he hastened to assure her. "I can't understand why Bob didn't tell me there were no men helping you." Rance hesitated, but then continued quietly, "Jim and Gail told me at Christmas time when they first saw me about the wedding. All they said was that they were concerned about an old friend of his who had made mischief by telling Gail he was secretly engaged to her. He wondered if he should confront her. It didn't take much to put two and two together, but they didn't mention you by name."

"Big of them!" She stared at him defiantly.

His face softened, and he said very gently, "It's very hard to face up to our failures, isn't it? Let alone accept them!"

Suddenly, the pain and misery of all the long months overwhelmed her. "Failures? What would you know about being a failure? Oh, I know everything there is to know about being a failure! Failing to win Jim is only the last of a very long list." She laughed harshly and without mirth. "Failing to be the soft, gentle, domesticated female—the daughter my mother always wanted. Failing to complete the science degree at university. Failing to have boy friends.

Failing to be like all the other soppy, hypocritical Christian women at church. . ." Her voice rose hysterically. "And telling outright lies is just what could be expected from a failure! Well, isn't it?" The tears started streaming down her face.

"I sincerely hope not," she heard him mutter. He sighed deeply.

Warm hands grasped Hilda gently by the shoulders. And then her trembling body was being held firmly against him. His shoulder was just the right height for her aching head, and she leaned into him as the sobs shook her.

Hilda didn't know how long he held her, soothing her with a soft hand on her back and murmuring comforting words. It was the first time she had really let go, not wanting to upset her father any more than he had been. When the sobs died down, she pushed away from him. He released her, produced a handkerchief, and started mopping her up.

She numbly let him wipe her saturated face, but when he held it to her nose and ordered her matter of factly to "blow," she found herself giving a choked sound and snatching it off him. He stood silently until she had finished. Then she felt his warm gentle fingers enclose her face. Reluctantly she raised her wet eyes.

"You're. . .you're very kind. . ." she faltered.

"Kind!"

Her eyes widened at the bleak expression that filled his face.

There was a wealth of self-contempt in his face and voice as he continued, "No, I'm not being kind. My old girl friend could certainly have told you she didn't think I was kind. And you're very wrong about my not knowing about being a failure, Hildie, my dear."

His voice was harsh. Hilda stared at him and took a step back. Deep in his dark eyes was a depth of anguish that more than matched her own.

"I'm perhaps one of the worst failures there is." His voice choked, and she watched with fascination as he swallowed painfully. "My mother believes I've failed as a son. I'm failing as a father. I've failed in my relationship with the woman I asked to marry me, and. . . and. . ." His voice sank even further, and Hilda had to strain to hear him. "I've failed as a minister of the gospel of Jesus Christ."

two

Hilda stood frozen as Rance stooped, picked up the small bag he had dropped, and strode past her. He wrenched the screen door open, and stood holding it for her.

"Let's get to bed," she heard him say wearily. "I've got to get up early to finish preparing for tomorrow's service."

She moved slowly toward him, and then stopped. "Mr. Telford, what do you mean, you—"

"Oh, Hildie, call me Rance," he said impatiently, "And I shouldn't have said what I did to you. I don't want to talk about it. Now, let's call it a night. We can talk more tomorrow. And about your problems, not mine," he added sharply."

Hilda hesitated for a moment, but he looked her in the eye and glared at her so angrily, she strode past him quickly. After she had briefly shown him to his room, he muttered an abrupt goodnight and closed the door firmly in her face.

She stared with amazement at the closed door. He hadn't even let her offer him some supper. Never had she known he could be like this! What on earth did he mean? The quiet, unassuming, respected Reverend Telford a failure?

Her shoulders slumped wearily as she turned away and automatically began switching off the lights before heading for her own room. At least he knew the lay-out of the rest of the house and could get a drink if he wanted anything. They had been on the church roster to provide meals for him and his fiancée at various times, but he had never stayed overnight with them before.

Hilda knew he was actually employed by a large church in Toowoomba. They had made an arrangement with the small bush church on the Darling Downs to release him to preach there once a month and do any other services for the smaller congregation as needed.

With a sigh of relief that the long day was at last over, she entered her bedroom and went over to close the curtains at her window. As she reached for the cord she paused and then frowned.

Come to think of it, when was the last time his fiancée, Maree Sadler, had been with Rance? Why, she couldn't remember seeing her since those busy harvest days well before Christmas. Suddenly she realized that it must have been about then he started accepting offers from various members of the church to stay overnight.

As Hilda prepared for bed, she acknowledged with a sense of shame that she had been so absorbed in her own misery and guilt that she had never once enquired about Maree, even though Rance had visited them quite a lot lately. Not that Hilda had ever liked his tall, sophisticated fiancée very much. Maree had never actually been unfriendly, just rather cool and aloof.

The last few weeks, Hilda had come in from the paddock several times to find Rance with her father. He had always left soon after, and she had taken for granted he had been keen to get home to his beautiful fiancée.

It wasn't until she was in bed that she remembered he had also said he'd failed as a father and a son. She shook her head. She must have heard incorrectly. She could understand only too well how he could feel he had not lived up to his mother's expectations, but how could he be a father when to her knowledge he had never been married? Her eyes widened. Unless of course. . .

She suddenly realized how little she really knew about Rance Telford. He had shared briefly once in a sermon that when he had accepted Christ as his Saviour while at university, he had been saved from a wasted life by the grace and power of Christ. He really wasn't much older than Jim, and his handsome, dark blonde looks had caused quite a stir among the girls at church until he had produced a fiancée.

She puzzled about it for awhile, and then decided if she was going to have to spend time with him tomorrow, she had better ask her father if he knew why Rance had been so abrupt and blurted out what he had. Then sheer exhaustion sent her into a deep sleep.

&

"Hildie! Rise and shine or you'll be late!" As he knocked sharply, Bob Garrett's voice rang cheerfully outside her door.

Hilda jerked awake and glanced at the clock. She groaned.

"I'm leaving in a few minutes with Rance to unlock the church and set up. See you when you get there, sleepy head!"

As she sprang out of bed, she heard his footsteps moving quickly away and then the faint murmur of voices. There was only time for a very quick cup of hot, steaming tea to wake her up properly before having a quick wash and scrambling into a cool shirtwaister cotton dress.

She scowled at her pale face and the bruises under her eyes and wished fervently that she could stay home. But, as long as she could remember, they had gone to Easter services as a family, and it would upset her father considerably if she did not turn up.

Make-up could not be neglected this morning or everyone would think she had gone into mourning! The eye shadow and touch of blusher she hurriedly applied helped. The white dress emphasized the dark golden tan of her neck and arms that had deepened from her hours on the tractor.

Satisfied at last, she glanced at her watch and groaned. Grabbing her bag, she raced down to the garage. She fervently hoped there would be a spare seat in the back row, or she would have to feel all those eyes on her as she walked down the front. It wasn't until the neat weatherboard building came into view that she realized she would now have very little opportunity of asking her father about Rance.

The church was comfortably full, and Hilda reluctantly had to take a seat almost near the front. Fortunately, Rance rose to his feet as she moved rapidly down the aisle, and attention was diverted to him as the rustling and murmurs were hushed.

She watched Rance with new eyes as his gaze swept over the congregation, welcoming them all to this Good Friday service. For the first time she noticed that he had lost weight, and the lines near his mouth were surely more marked.

"Let us take another look at the cross, this morning," she suddenly realized he was saying in a quiet voice. "Let us look at the battered, bruised Man hanging on that cruel thing, suffering the taunts and jibes of His enemies, and remember this is our God there, in human form, suffering and dying in your place and mine."

Then he announced the first hymn, and the organ began playing very softly. Hilda glanced across at her father. This was one of his favourites, and suddenly she was fiercely proud of him, loving him as the music swelled and they stood to sing. She knew how softly he would throb out the first and second verses of "When I Survey the Wondrous

Cross," and how the third would be a little louder, and how he loved to boom out that last triumphant declaration of commitment and love.

The tears were burning her eyes by the time the voices reverently, but loudly, started that last verse, pouring out the faith and commitment of the people. Her own voice choked with tears as she realized what she was singing as she never had before. God's demand on her life was that she give Him complete control of every aspect. How she had failed to do that!

She looked up swiftly. Rance's loud, rich tones had faltered, and faded to a complete stop. His eyes were fixed on the hymnbook in front of him. Then he moved jerkily, and she saw his hand clench tightly on the edge of the lectern. The triumphant voices and music finished together, and for a moment there was absolute stillness.

Hilda's eyes remained fixed on Rance. He opened his mouth and then closed it again, swallowing convulsively. "Let us join in prayer," he managed huskily at last with an obvious effort.

As the heads bowed around her, Hilda continued to stare worriedly at him. One lean hand passed over his mouth and she heard him clear his throat. He then clasped his hands very tightly in front of him and briefly and simply asked God to bless each one present and accept their worship and praise. Hilda was still staring at him as he said a fervent "amen."

As she sat down with the rest of the people, she felt guilty—and rather foolish—that she had not really heard what he had prayed!

Hilda found herself suddenly offering up a brief, earnest prayer for Rance. Whatever had happened to cause his anguish, so briefly revealed to her the night before, had not stopped him from serving the church this weekend. She had just caught a brief glimpse of the effort it was costing him to remain calm, clear headed, and stand up there in front of them all.

Whatever he thought of himself, whether he was actually the failure he claimed or not, suddenly a wave of admiration for his strength and dedication swept through her. If he really believed he was failing in all those areas, her own problems suddenly seemed minimal in comparison.

But when Hilda was standing waiting for her father after the service, those same problems surfaced savagely and she began to wish she had stayed home after all. A few folk wished her a quiet good morning, but she sensed many others weren't quite sure how to greet her. A pair of young teenage girls were obviously avidly curious about how she was taking the wedding the following day. Then a couple she knew very well walked right past her as though she was invisible and joined the crowd of well wishers around Jim and Gail.

Her feelings raw, she turned away and spotted Beth hurrying toward her. She started to smile with relief at her old friend, but froze as Beth merely nodded tight-lipped at her before hurrying past to grab her two small children, Jacky and Robbie.

"She'll get over it, Hildie," a deep, compassionate voice murmured softly behind her. "She's very worried about her husband at the moment."

Hilda kept her face averted. "Beth hasn't spoken to me since . . . since. . . ." Then what Rance had said sank in and she turned abruptly to him. "Worried about Arthur? I thought he was doing very well since they moved to Brisbane," she said anxiously.

Those compassionate eyes studied her thoughtfully for a

moment, and then softened even more. "I saw him a couple of weeks ago at their house in Brisbane. He's going through another bout of depression. I didn't really get a fantastic welcome!" A wry smile crossed his face. "Told me bluntly just because he still can't walk it means he suddenly wants anything to do with religion!"

The thought of Beth's rough diamond of a husband being suddenly confronted by a visit from Beth's home church minister brought a touch of amusement to Hilda's strained face. "And I suspect he didn't say it quite as politely as that to you!"

Rance laughed. "You suspect right!" Then he sobered, and sighed. "If ever a man needed to have a personal relationship with the Lord to get him through each day, Arthur does."

"Oh, dear, his paralysis isn't worse, is it?" Hilda asked anxiously.

"No, no," Rance hastened to reassure her. "He's still getting about in his wheelchair okay. But he's still not reconciled to being so dependant." He smiled ruefully. "I don't suppose I'd handle being partially paralysed from the waist down very well either."

Before Hilda could respond, she noticed her father approaching. "Rance, I'm going to take Dad home," she said hurriedly, "He looks so tired!"

"Right," he agreed briskly, "I'll see you both later after I've locked up."

But by the time he arrived at the farm, only Hilda greeted him. "I insisted Dad go and lie down," she said to him quickly as he entered the kitchen where she had just finished serving out a cold meal for them both. "Afraid our picnic is off," she added abruptly. "I don't want to leave him."

Rance looked concerned. "I tried to get him to let me bring someone from town to play for at least today, but he insisted he'd manage."

"I tried too," Hilda said grimly, "but my father has always done exactly what he wanted to when it comes to playing his music!"

They shared the meal almost in silence. And yet, it wasn't an uncomfortable silence, Hilda mused as she ventured a glance at him from time to time. A few times his lips were a straight line and his expression so grim, that she knew his thoughts were a long way from the peaceful farm house. She was still feeling weary and concerned enough about her father not to be interested in talking too much, even to bring up their conversation of the night before.

However, to their immense relief, after a few hours, Bob Garrett declared he was fine and insisted on joining them for the evening meal and then a game of Scrabble later. His colour was much improved, and Hilda found rather to her own astonishment that she enjoyed the fun of Rance and herself being thoroughly beaten by him.

"Well!" Rance declared rather wistfully as Bob gleefully added up their scores, "It's a long time since I enjoyed a game of Scrabble. Especially so well-matched!"

"Well-matched? Against this old rogue!" laughed Hilda, "He's always coming up with words I've never even heard! And you had a few yourself. I think you're just a pair of cheats!"

Rance's eyes danced, but he intoned piously, "Oh, no, never let it be said of two Christian gentlemen. We just read the right kind of books!"

"Yeah," she laughed back at him, "real heavy old theological tomes!"

"Tomes! Now that's a word I could have used—"

Rance and Hilda groaned together. Bob Garrett stopped and then laughed with them.

"No more!" chuckled Hilda. "I need some supper. Any takers?"

Both men chorused their approval cheerfully, but as Hilda bustled off to the kitchen, she missed seeing the thumbs up sign her suddenly grave-faced father gave his friend behind her back. Rance nodded with a slight, sympathetic smile. When Hilda returned they started teasing her, and it was with some satisfaction they eventually said goodnight to her prettily flushed, smiling face.

For some reason Hilda found it hard to explain to herself, the wedding the next day was not the traumatic time she had expected. Perhaps it was because the sheer radiance of the bride and groom left little space for regret and dwelling on "the might have beens." Perhaps it was because Hilda found herself watching Rance with new eyes again.

He had really relaxed last night, and been good fun. She had never before seen him as an ordinary man, and not in his position as "the minister." Whatever had made him blurt out his belief that he had failed as a minister, she could see no sign of that as he led the marriage service.

As she watched him smiling lovingly at the pair before him, it suddenly struck Hilda that he was a very good minister, indeed. She thought of the favourable comments she had heard expressed about him by folk he had visited in their homes when they had been facing difficult times.

"He has a pastor's heart, that one. He really cares," she had overheard said by an elderly gentleman, who had been in the throes of the heartache of having to leave his farm to live in the city. His listeners had chorused their enthusiastic agreement.

Although he had always given her the impression of being a quietly spoken, gentle man, the sermons Rance had preached with fire and passion had often made her wince, and stirred her up to determine to be a better Christian.

But my good intentions didn't amount to much, she thought bitterly, forcing a smile as her father glanced at her.

The wedding reception was being held at a large hall in the small township of Cecil Plains, about half an hour's drive from the church. Hilda drove slowly, reluctant to arrive too early.

Her father was quiet also, absorbed in his own thoughts, until he said suddenly, "Hilda, after the wedding, I. . .I have to tell you something."

His voice sounded so strained that she glanced at him sharply. "Are you sure you're up to going to the reception, Dad? I could take you home, and then return myself. I know everyone would understand."

"No, no," he said swiftly, "I am a bit tired again, but my part's finished now and I'll just sit quietly. It's just. . ." He paused, and then added steadily, "I've been talking a lot to Rance lately about something that happened a long time ago. . .a very long time ago. Ever since your. . .your mother died I've been wondering whether I should tell you. He's convinced me that you have a right to know."

"Goodness, Dad, what deep, dark secrets could you have?" Hilda said with a smile as she glanced fondly at him. Then she saw the way he was sitting rigidly in his seat, his hands clutched together. "Dad! What on earth?"

He turned and caught her worried expression. "No, not now!" he interrupted her sharply. "Later. I just had to put the decision I've made into words so I don't chicken out again. We haven't enough time now. It's kept all these years.

Another few hours won't matter."

Hilda bit her tongue, stifling the questions that began to seethe. She had always known that her parents' relationship had not always been rosy. Her mother had been a very fussy, nervous person who could suddenly erupt over seemingly trivial things that displeased her.

And then in her early teens, Hilda had realized there was something important in her past she had not wanted her daughter to know. One time when she had overheard them arguing, her mother had become almost hysterical, screaming at her father that he was not to tell Hilda. As had happened so many times, he had given way to the small woman whom Hilda had always known he loved more than anyone, even his own daughter.

"You. . .you've grown very close to Rance, haven't you, Dad?" Hilda said quietly after a long, tense silence.

There was another silence for a moment, and then Bob Garrett muttered, "He's a man with an immense problem to sort out, Hildie, love. Maree couldn't cope with it and broke off her engagement to him last year."

"Broke off their engagement! But why didn't you tell me? Does anyone else know?"

"No!" he said sharply, "and he doesn't want it broadcast just yet. He had to tell the leaders of the church in Toowoomba about it all, but he doesn't want the folk here to know until a decision has been made about—"

Bob Garrett broke off and drew in a sharp breath even as Hilda slowed the car to turn into the carpark. "But it's not my prerogative to talk about that. We've been doing a lot of praying and sharing the Word together to help him find his way. Things still aren't resolved for him by any means, but I think it's me who's at last found my way."

He was silent as the car rolled to a stop, and then smiled

gently at the worried, bewildered face Hilda turned towards him. "Hildie, daughter-dear. . ." He reached over and touched her gently on her nose with his forefinger in the familiar way he had as long as she could remember. "I. . .I . . .you know that I've always loved you very, very much, don't you?"

She nodded, her throat choked up with emotion. He had not called her his "daughter-dear" for a long time. Then the grave expression on his face was blurred by the sudden mist that covered her eyes, as the usually undemonstrative man leaned over and kissed her gently on the forehead.

Before Hilda had got over her absolute astonishment, her father was out of the car and calling out to folk who had also just arrived. She followed him slowly, trying to behave as though the last few moments had not happened.

As the hours passed, Hilda joined in the festive activities of the reception as best she could. She had to force herself to eat the delicious meal, though, and constantly found her eyes drawn to where Rance was seated at the head table. Her thoughtswere in turmoil. They swung from Rance to her father's unusual behaviour and back again.

There was a burst of laughter from the bridal party, and Hilda glanced across at them automatically, her thoughts still worrying over her fathers words. What could he possibly need to tell her that distressed him so much?

"Hildie!" her father suddenly whispered savagely. "Stop scowling, and at least give the impression of having a good time! You'll spoil the day for Jim and Gail."

Hilda turned to him in astonishment.

"People are watching you," he added under his breath, and then turned to the people on his other side and engaged them in conversation.

Hilda felt the hot tide of red that swept into her face, and applied herself to the food in front of her, not game to look up. She'd hardly given a thought to the bride and groom! It was the minister taking all her attention, she realized with something like a touch of horror.

She turned a little desperately to the middle-aged lady seated on her other side and engaged her in inane conversation. Afterwards, she could never remember even the woman's name, and certainly nothing that they had talked about.

When the delicious pavlova with its topping of fresh strawberries, kiwi fruit, banana, and whipped cream was served, Hilda noticed that her father had hardly touched the roast lamb and vegetables of the first course. But his face was animated and he was enjoying himself, she told herself, trying to stifle the pang of fear for him.

She wondered briefly again what it was he had decided to tell her. Probably some old skeleton in the cupboard from his past or, more likely, her mother's. Her parents had never talked very much about the days before she had been born. Her mother had been well into her forties when Hilda had made her appearance, and they had told her many times over the years what a difference her late arrival in their marriage had made.

So it was that, when the master of ceremonies called for quiet and the usual speeches commenced, it was with a small sense of shock that Hilda realized she had hardly thought of Jim and Gail as actually being married.

Hilda studied Jim thoughtfully when it came his turn to stand up and respond. He was certainly a very handsome man. He was also a very nice man, a good friend to have. She glanced back at Rance. He was watching her intently, and for a moment their eyes locked. Then his beautiful, kind smile transformed his face, and she found her own lips twitching in response.

Suddenly it was as though a tremendous burden rolled from her, and her tentative smile became a sudden beam. She saw Rance straighten and the smile was wiped off his face. Hilda looked quickly back at Jim, feeling suddenly ridiculously shy.

She knew with sudden clarity that a part of her would always love Jim, but as the brother she had never had. He had been so right about their relationship all along.

As Jim sat down and Hilda joined in the enthusiastic clapping, she glanced at Gail and found her looking at her a little anxiously. Hilda found herself smiling a little mistily and apologetically at her. She saw Gail catch her breath slightly. Then suddenly Gail's whole face lit up as she smiled radiantly back at her.

Message received and understood.

The rest of the evening passed in something of a blur for Hilda. What stood out much later was the feeling of utter relief she had felt as she hugged Gail good-bye. The bride had changed out of the breathtakingly beautiful lace wedding gown into a smart suit and had topped her shining, honey blonde curls with a frivolous piece of net that could have been called a hat.

Hilda had murmured a fervent, "I'm so sorry, Gail," and received an extra generous hug and kiss of understanding from the radiant bride. Jim had beamed at her with relief and given her one of his old brotherly hugs, before passing on to the next well wisher to say good-bye. Then they had driven off noisily in Jim's Holden. It had been decorated with tin cans and all kinds of weird and wonderful things by Jim's young brother, Will, and some of his friends.

But all of that was overshadowed and wiped away when the touch on Hilda's arm made her turn a laughing face from watching the departing car toward Rance Telford. Something clutched her heart when she saw his pale face and anxious expression.

Then she knew, even as he spoke.

"Hildie, dear, it's your Dad. He's not at all well. Complaining of chest pain. Jean Drew's with him. We're organising a car to get him to the doctor."

"Oh, no, oh, no," she moaned continually as she rushed back inside.

But she was too late.

Bob Garrett was no longer breathing. His face was grey. Jean Drew, a very experienced nursing sister, had already started cardiac pulmonary resuscitation. Rance raced to join her, but it was to no avail.

The father Hilda had loved so dearly all her life had gone Home for eternity with his best Friend.

three

In direct contrast to the warm sunny weather of the Easter weekend just past, the day of the funeral was overcast and cold, a reminder that winter was not too far away.

Hilda had come out of her anguished daze enough that first evening to state vehemently to a devastated Marian Stevens that Jim and Gail were not to be told. It would only spoil their honeymoon, and she had already caused them enough heartache. At that, Rance's beautiful, gentle smile had briefly reached through to the part of her that had frozen. It brought some semblance of warmth, but she had turned away from him.

Rance had never been far away that first night. Dry-eyed, Hilda had wandered aimlessly around the house and then outside to sit with Polly crouched close beside her, until Rance had at last persuaded her to lie down in her room.

Later she realized that Jean Drew had been there with them too, preparing the endless cups of tea and then the supper she had not been able to swallow for the lump in her throat. She had bowed her head when they prayed with her, but not even prayer had penetrated her pain. God seemed far away.

During the long two days that had slipped by, Hilda functioned on some automatic level of rigid self-control. She was vaguely aware that people were being very kind. Jean Drew had moved in and stayed night and day with her. Rance had come and gone, and then had slept at the house again on Easter Monday before the funeral the next day.

He had gently organized everything, asking her wishes, but she had let him make all the arrangements, only requesting they sing the hymn from Good Friday, "When I Survey the Wondrous Cross."

The funeral was held in the little building her father had worshipped and served in all his life. Rance had offered to organize it in the bigger city church, but she had refused.

"There. . .there aren't any relatives who can come, Rance," she had faltered dry-eyed, feeling so dreadfully alone. "There's only Great-Aunt Lily, my mother's aunt. And she's in a nursing home in Sydney. We. . .we never kept in touch with any of her family. So there won't be a lot of people. And he. . .he. . .this was the place he loved . . ."

Rance had looked at her a little strangely, but made no comment.

In fact, Hilda was amazed at the number who came to say their last farewell to their friend, neighbour, and brother in Christ. There were far more folk than at her mother's funeral. Only when the crowd spilled out of the packed little church did Hilda realize Rance had been wiser than she by quietly contacting someone to set up amplification outside so the overflow could hear.

Rance spoke with conviction about the resurrection and the hope of the Christian. Hilda had heard it all before at her mother's funeral. Then she had been strengthened and comforted. But now she just felt cold, and nothing that was said touched her. As she steeled herself to composedly accept the hugs and tears afterwards, it was as though it was happening to someone else. It couldn't possibly be her darling father they were referring to.

And Jim and Gail were present. They had returned from

their honeymoon at the Goldcoast after all. "We loved him, too," a sad-eyed Jim said briefly. "Mum had to tell us."

Jean Drew continued to stay with Hilda the rest of the week. Despite the older woman's protests, Hilda insisted on starting up the tractor the day after the funeral. Rance had gone back to Toowoomba straight from the funeral, causing Hilda to feel as though he had deserted her. She felt vaguely surprised how much she missed his quiet, accepting presence.

It had not rained as expected, and the days warmed up again. In fact it had become very hot and humid for April, and Hilda turned on the car's air conditioner as she drove herself and Jean to the Sunday morning service the following weekend.

"I'm glad there's not a lot of paddocks left to cultivate," Hilda observed, as a trickle of sweat ran down her face. "This hot weather will surely bring the rain."

"Perhaps," said Jean quietly. "But you've nearly exhausted yourself doing it."

"It. . .it's what Dad would have wanted," Hilda said just as quietly, but with clipped words. She added quickly, "We'll probably get a thunderstorm this evening if this keeps up."

"Bob would not like to see how pale and drawn you are, my dear," Jean persisted.

Hilda's grip on the steering wheel tightened. The car swerved a little, and Jean glanced at her sharply.

"I wish you'd let me drive, Hilda."

"And I told you I could manage perfectly well!" Hilda snapped irritably. Then she swallowed painfully on the hard lump that seemed to have taken up permanent residence in her throat. "I. . .I'm sorry, Aunt Jean. I. . .you didn't deserve that," she murmured with shame.

When Jean didn't answer, Hilda felt worse. Jean had gently suggested that morning that it might be too soon for Hilda to face everyone at church, offering to share a simple time of fellowship with her at home. Hilda had simply stared at her in surprise. Dad would have expected her to go. But ever since the tentative warning, Hilda had felt the tension building up in her, and now she wondered if Jean might have been right after all.

"It's good to hear you call me 'aunt' again, child," the older woman said softly at last. "I've always been especially fond of you over the years."

There was a faint tremor in her voice, and Hilda bit her lip. It had only been the last year or so that Hilda had felt it was too babyish to keep on using the honorary title the three friends had long ago bestowed on this old friend of the Stevens family. She had never married, and to Hilda's knowledge had no close family. Never before had Jean made any comment on being just called 'Jean.'

One of the senior men of the congregation led the service and preached that morning. The first hymn had hardly commenced when Hilda knew that Jean had been right. It was too soon to sit in this familiar place with a strange face occupying the seat at the organ.

Hilda sat rigidly during the long hour that followed. She found she dared not open her mouth to sing, and she couldn't pray. Immediately after the benediction, she was immensely relieved when Jean grasped her arm and hurried her from the building before anyone could do more than smile sympathetically at her desperate, strained face. Without a word, Jean held out her hand for the car keys, climbed into the driver's seat, and drove them quickly home.

Hilda's rigid self-control lasted until they stopped at the house. As Rance's familiar figure rose from the old chair on the verandah, the volcano of emotions seething inside her erupted. It never entered her mind until a long time later to wonder why he was there and not at his church service in Toowoomba.

She sprang out of the car and slammed the door viciously. Jean followed her hurriedly. Hilda ignored Jean's tentative, "Hilda, dear. . ." and strode angrily up the steps to the quiet figure waiting for them.

"It's not fair! It's not fair!" she stormed. "Why did he have to go and leave me too? He said he loved me. If he did, why did he leave me like that? Why! Why! I. . .I didn't even have time to say good-bye. There's no one else, now. No. . .one. What am I going to do?"

Her tight fists were thumping on Rance's solid, muscular chest. She felt her knees suddenly buckle. Then she felt strong arms sweep up her shaking body. She buried her head against his warmth, clutching wildly at him. As she felt him turn and carry her inside, she heard Jean's tearful voice saying from a distance, "I've been afraid of something like this."

But then the wracking sobs came at last. Hilda cried as though she would never stop. Vaguely she realized warm arms cradled her. Rance's cracked, broken voice tried to soothe her. Moisture touched her face from his as she clung to him.

There was a faint murmur of voices. Rance moved, and she felt the soft mattress beneath her. The protective arms left her and she curled into a tight ball of agony, feeling desperately alone once more.

Rance's choked voice whispered, "God's here, sweetheart. He's loving you." Then a large gentle hand pushed her tumbled hair away from her face, and stroked and soothed her.

Rance murmured something she couldn't quite hear over his shoulder to Jean, something about someone dying. There was a shocked exclamation, and then a woman's voice, like Jean's and yet not like Jean's. Briefly it broke through the pain that wracked Hilda. It was filled with such emotion. . . praying. . . .

"Oh, loving God! Oh, Father! Be near and bring these tortured hearts Your comfort and Your peace. . ." The tearful voice continued to pray softly, but Hilda's sobs drowned out the words. Timeless moments later, Hilda's agony gradually died away and her exhausted body slept.

When Hilda at last stirred, for a moment she wondered why her eyes felt so sticky as she opened them, and why she had gone to bed in her clothes. Then she remembered, and gave a deep, quivering sigh. It was real. Her father really was dead.

There was a rustle of movement, and a quiet voice asked, "Would you like a hot drink, Hilda, dear?"

Hilda peered up at Jean. As the older woman's tender hand pushed back a heavy lock of dark hair away from her face, she suddenly remembered the feel of a larger, stronger hand, and pushed herself up on one elbow, glancing swiftly around the room. "I. . .I'm sorry, Aunt Jean, I. . ."

"I'm not, love. Tears are one of God's precious gifts. We've been so worried because until now there weren't any."

Hilda sat up slowly. Tears burnt behind her eyes again, but suddenly she knew Jean was right. Her head ached a little but that hard lump in her throat had dissolved. Although that crushed, helpless feeling was not completely gone, it was definitely a lot easier.

She looked around the room again. "Did. . .did I dream it, or was Rance really here?" she asked huskily.

Jean turned away quickly. "Yes, he stayed as long as he could, but he had to go. Some. . .some urgent matters were waiting for him. I'll get that drink for you. And you must be hungry," she finished a little abruptly before disappearing through the doorway.

Hilda swept her hair back from her face and swung her legs over the side of the bed. She frowned, disappointed that Rance had gone again so soon. There had been so much she needed to talk to him about.

For the first time since the wedding reception, Hilda actually enjoyed the food that Jean set before them that evening.

"It's good to see you with some colour back in your cheeks," Jean said with a hint of buoyancy in her voice as she smiled gently at her. Then her expression changed. "Hilda, I'm very sorry, but I'm afraid my holidays from the hospital finish in another few days."

Hilda looked up at her blankly, and Jean added hurriedly, "I was going to ask for an extension of my leave in the morning. But now I'm wondering if you think you'll be able to cope on your own. Marian said she could come over for a few hours most days for awhile, but she has Will to think of, and the farm, while Jim's away.

Hilda reached across the table and took Jean's hand. "Oh, Aunt Jean, I don't know what I'd have done without you this last week." Tears choked her for a moment, but she resolutely forced them back. "I just haven't been thinking straight since. . .since. . ."

"Yes, yes, I know that, dear," Jean assured her quickly, "but there are certain business matters as. . .as well as other things that you need to think about, aren't there? Marian said to tell you that when you're ready, she'll help you all she can. She went through this when her husband died, and she'll be able to advise you."

"Oh," Hilda said blankly, "yes, of course. I. . .I suppose there's the bank, and. . .and Dad's will. He. . .he. . ." She fought for control.

"Now, now," Jean said rapidly, "don't worry about it anymore tonight. Try and get some more rest. We'll talk about things tomorrow."

But much later that night, after they had gone to their bedrooms, Hilda couldn't sleep, and eventually turned on the light again and started making a list of all the things she could think of that would need attention in the days ahead. The list grew ominously long. She had not ventured into her father's bedroom since he had gone. There were her father's clothes, his personal papers, his war plane collection, bills to pay. . .

The tears crept down her cheeks again. "Oh, God, I need You!" she suddenly cried aloud. "Where's the comfort and the peace You're supposed to give at times like this to someone who believes in You?" she accused angrily.

She flung herself down on the pillow, and a flood of tears came again. Impatient with herself, she sat up after a while, fighting for control. Reaching for another tissue from the box on her bedside table, her hand bumped the book lying there. With a quivering sob, her fingers closed on it and she picked it up.

The burgundy leather cover was thick with dust. With a sense of shame she wiped it off. Since her father had been sick there had been so much to do that there had seemed no time to even have a token daily reading of her Bible. She rubbed at her wet cheeks and then she opened the book at random. It fell open at a bookmark. The words on it sprang out at her.

"Underneath are the everlasting arms."

She gave a soft sob and turned it over, knowing what she would see. A few days before her mother had died after her long illness, her father had given it to her. On the back he had written, "My daughter-dear, always let Him hold you safe in His loving arms too."

She cradled the Bible in her arms. It was almost like a rebuke directly from her father. She was crying out for help, but until now had not gone to the Source of all help and strength. She had not even opened up the Scriptures, or spent time on her knees.

In fact, she couldn't remember really spending time alone with the Lord since she had lied to Gail. Somehow it had seemed as though her prayers had bounced off the ceiling. And now, because of the faithful teaching she had been given by her parents and through the church fellowship, she knew deep down in her being what the problem was. It was only unconfessed sin that hindered her prayers and had taken away her desire to read the Scriptures.

With a sob of regret and pain, she tumbled out of bed and onto her knees. "I'm so sorry, Lord. I've been so nasty and horrible. . .and. . .and I've lied, and. . .Oh, please forgive me. Oh, Lord, I do so need to feel Your arms about me now more than I ever have," she murmured fervently.

A few more tears slipped silently down her face. She gave a deep sigh and felt herself relax.

Many times down the years she would remember those next few moments with a sense of awed wonder. The sense of God's presence was suddenly so real, so close, that it was as though He wrapped her up in His arms. She was never to forget the awareness of a great Love surrounding her. And with it came peace and the first sound, dreamless sleep for many long days.

More gentle, healing tears were shed in the next few days

while doing all that had to be done. But each night in her room, Hilda opened the Scriptures and read and prayed and grasped hold of the promises she read with single-minded fervour.

"You've been really wonderful, Hilda," Jean said briskly the morning she said good-bye. "We're very proud of you."

Hilda smiled a little self-consciously at her. She knew that the "we" included Marian Stevens who had spent many hours helping out. All constraint between them was now a thing of the past.

"Hilda," Jean added a little hesitantly, "while you were outside with Polly this morning, Rance rang. He. . .he wanted to know how you were and to tell you he's sorry he hasn't been in contact with you."

Hilda refused to acknowledge even to herself just how disappointed she had been that she had not seen or even heard from him since Sunday, so she shrugged nonchalantly, and merely said, "I guess he's been busy." Before Jean could refer to him again, Hilda reached out and gave her a big hug. "Thank's so much for everything, Aunt Jean. I don't know what I'd have done without you."

"Rubbish, my dear. I wish I could have stayed and done more," Jean said a little unsteadily. "Your Dad was a very fine man. I've known him a long time and I'm going to miss him, too, you know. Now, don't forget," she added rapidly as she straightened, "let me know any time you can plan a trip to Sydney. I'd love to see you."

The house was quiet and empty after Marian had driven away with Jean. Hilda went for a stroll down to the sheds. She poked around the large machinery shed, mentally noting jobs still not attended to. Then she suddenly realized she had not seen Polly all morning.

She called and whistled, and when no collie came bounding out, her heart missed a beat. Anxiously she moved over to the small garden shed near the house. Here the dog always settled for the night beside her bowl of water and food dish. She called loudly again, and a surge of relief filled her when the collie appeared in the doorway.

"Oh, Polly, you had me worried there for a moment," she exclaimed with relief as she knelt to hug and pet the animal. To her relief the lump on the nose didn't appear to be any larger, but the dog seemed much quieter as Hilda let her inside the house and fussed over her.

"We'd better get you to the vet, I'm afraid," Hilda muttered anxiously. She thought for a moment and then went to the phone.

The vet she normally went to was out of town, but had a late appointment free the next day. After she had hung up, Hilda hesitated, and then picked up the phone again and tried Rance Telford's number. Perhaps she could call in and see him while she was in Toowoomba.

As she heard the ringing tone, sudden heat flooded through her as she remembered the way she had flown at him. And then she remembered also that his tears had mingled with her own, and she felt comforted knowing he too had thought very highly of her father. Suddenly, Hilda was fiercely grateful that he had spent so much time with her father so recently. Her father had enjoyed his company so much.

No one answered, and her disappointment was more than she had expected. She frowned at herself as she hung up and took Polly outside to give her long hair a good brush.

At first it had been too painful to dwell on that last precious day with her father. Now she let her thoughts linger on events the day of the wedding. Suddenly she remembered what her father had told her about Rance Telford and his fiancée, or rather, ex-fiancée. Her hand paused in its rhythmic brushing.

Polly objected, and lifted a paw to Hilda's lap. For once, Hilda didn't smile and make her usual fuss of the dog. She resumed the brushing automatically as concern for Rance filled her.

He had been really down. Called himself a failure. Her hand paused briefly again. More than that, he had also said something about failing as a father. She dismissed his claim of failing as a minister, although to feel so, that undoubtedly dedicated man must have been feeling very down. Hadn't her father said Maree Sadler had broken off their engagement because of some immense problem Rance had that she could not cope with?

Hilda gave in to Polly's short bark of displeasure that expressive paw treatment had failed to re-start the soothing brushing. But as her hand continued to untangle the dog's long hair, her mind was still with the man who had somehow begun to occupy so much of her thoughts.

Rance must have been married before, or else. . .or else their minister, who had often warned the young people about letting their boy-girl relationships get out of hand outside of marriage, might have known what he was talking about from bitter experience. She wondered sympathetically if the problem her Dad had mentioned had affected Rance in the ministry in Toowoomba.

Then, as she had many times these past few days, she pondered sadly about what her father could possibly have been going to tell her later that night. There had been no hint of anything in his private papers to give her a clue.

Her hands stilled. Polly nudged her again to continue, but this time the dog got no response. What if, Hilda mused, her father had told Rance?

"Where are you, Rance Telford?" she muttered crossly, acknowledging how disappointed she had been he had not visited her again. "Don't you know I've got so many questions you may be able to answer?"

References in the Scriptures about life, death, and the resurrection that she had never really studied in depth before, she badly wanted to ask Rance about. Now she admitted a little reluctantly that she also needed to see him again as much for his strength and compassion.

Marian rang that evening. On being told about the trip to Toowoomba she immediately offered to go with Hilda.

"No thanks, Aunt Marian," Hilda said gratefully. "I've also managed to get an appointment with Dad's solicitor." She hesitated, but for some reason she couldn't understand herself, she refrained from mentioning her intention to try and see Rance as well.

The appointment with the solicitor went smoothly. He assured her that her father's affairs were all in order and there would be no problems transferring everything over into her name. There would just be the usual numerous forms to fill out and government requirements to fulfill. It all seemed unreal, and Hilda was glad of the excuse to rush off to keep the appointment at the vet.

"It could be one of three things," the vet told her after examining Polly. "A simple infection which long-nosed animals are susceptible to, a fungal infection, or. . .or a tumour, I'm afraid."

An appointment was organized the next day for the dog to have tests under a general anaesthetic. A shaken Hilda gave Polly an extra hug once they were back in the car. "Oh, Polly, dear. It has to be just an infection. It has to!"

On an impulse, she decided to see if Rance happened to be home. The brick veneer house next to the old church on a busy road was easy to find with the sign "Church Manse" prominently displayed. She had never had cause to visit there before, and as she opened the small, wrought iron gate, she felt a tinge of disappointment at the ill-kept lawn and gardens. Surely the grounds of a minister's residence should be better maintained than this. In fact, the whole place looked deserted. She was disappointed, but not really surprised, when no one answered the door.

As she drove home into the setting sun she wondered if Rance was living somewhere else. She fervently hoped that he had someone to help him through his problems the way he and Jean Drew had been there for her.

The sun's legacy of pink-tinged clouds was fading rapidly, and the stars were starting to peep out as Hilda drove slowly up the long driveway from the road to her home. A slight feeling of panic touched her at the thought that from now on, she would be coming home to an empty house.

She did not bother to garage the car, pulling up near the house to let Polly out. It was only as she nearly reached the house herself that she simultaneously noticed a car parked down near the garage, and realized someone was waiting for her after all.

"Hello, Hildie. I hoped you'd be home tonight soon," familiar deep tones said to her from the verandah.

Her face lit up. "Oh, Rance. I'm so glad you're here! I just called to see you in Toowoomba."

She ran up the steps, and somehow both her hands were clasped tightly in his. And someone had called her "Hildie" again! In her early teenage years she had decided she absolutely hated her old-fashioned name. Her father had started calling her "Hildie" despite her mother's strong protests. And she had been "Hilda" for so long, people who had known her since birth never had become used to

"Hildie."

She heard Rance give a deep sigh of relief. "You're better."

The smile on her face wobbled a little. "Not. . .not completely, but I no longer feel so. . .so spaced out."

She was a little surprised at just how thrilled she was he had come to see her, and feeling a little embarrassed, she tugged her hands from his and moved past him to open the door. She switched on the lights and then threw down her handbag on the hall table as she heard him follow her inside.

"Have you had tea yet?" she asked over her shoulder on her way to the kitchen. When he didn't answer her, she turned toward him and then was still. "You look dreadful!" she whispered at last.

His face was pale and drawn. He obviously hadn't shaved that day, but worst of all were the red-rimmed, sunken eyes. He was wearing a crumpled, stained tee-shirt and a pair of battered jeans.

He gave a harsh, mirthless laugh. "I guess that's all part of the scene that goes along with your world falling around you. We seem to be in the same boat, don't we?" His eyes swept over her, and then returned to study her face. "It's good to see you're coping so much better. Have you come to terms now with the fact that you were adopted?"

Hilda stared at him speechlessly. She opened her mouth, and nothing came out. She tried again, even as she saw Rance's face change to an expression of horror.

"A. . .adopted?" she managed to croak. "Are. . .are you crazy?"

four

"He didn't tell you." Rance's voice was flat. He closed his eyes tightly for a moment. When he looked at her again, regret, bewilderment, a myriad of emotions had filled his pale face and red-rimmed eyes.

Neither moved.

Every drop of colour drained from Hilda's cheeks as she read the truth in his eyes. She forced her legs to move and almost fell into the nearest chair.

"I wonder if there's any other way to stuff up this week?" Rance muttered angrily.

His long strides took him past her. When he returned a moment later with a glass of water, he crouched down beside her. She was shaking so much he held the glass to her lips. Her teeth clattered briefly against the edge as she obediently swallowed a mouthful. Then suddenly she pushed his hand violently aside. The water sloshed over his hand and onto the carpet. He ignored it, holding her gaze steadily.

She searched his eyes pleadingly. Wordlessly.

"Your father told me he had decided to tell you. Or rather," Rance hastened to add rapidly, "he said he would try and tell you."

"He didn't." Hilda heard her voice as though it was coming from a vast distance. She shook her head slightly, and then rubbed one hand jerkily across her forehead. "On. . . on the way to the wedding. . . No, no. . .it was the reception." She stopped and tried to moisten her suddenly dry lips.

O God, O God, her mind screamed. *It's not true. . . It can't be. Help me!*

"He said he wanted to tell me something later," she said at last in a carefully controlled monotone. "He said it had happened so long ago, another few hours wouldn't make a difference." A sound—half laugh, half sob of anguish—tore from her. "He. . .he was wrong, wasn't he?"

"Oh, Hildie, I'm so sorry," Rance murmured brokenly.

"Tell. . .tell me. Please."

Rance didn't move for a moment. Then he stood up. Deliberately and carefully he turned away, putting the nearly empty glass on the table. He stood rigidly with his back turned to her.

"Did. . .did he tell you about Maree and. . .and Nathan?"

For a moment the switch in conversation confused her. Maree? Who was Nathan? What did they have to do with—?

"Did he tell you about our broken engagement?" he insisted more forcefully.

Hilda nodded, and then dazedly realized he couldn't see that, and moistened her lips again and managed to say "Yes."

She saw him straighten his shoulders and then turn slowly to face her. His expression was remote. "Have you told anyone else?" he asked sharply.

"Of course not!"

He relaxed a little, and then picked up a chair and moved it directly in front of her. "Thank you," he said simply as he sat down. "The church leaders in Toowoomba know now, but your father has been the only one I felt free to talk with about the whole situation." He looked down at his hands. "He was wonderful to me, and we grew very close. So much so, that one day when I was feeling particularly down, he told me he also had a problem he wanted to talk about. I think he was really trying to get me to come out of. . .of wallowing in self-pity."

Rance raised his head, and then reached over and picked up one of Hilda's hands with both of his. "He. . .he was very worried about his daughter-dear, whom he loved very much."

Hilda moved convulsively, and then was clinging wordlessly to Rance's hands.

"I felt very honoured when he said he had never spoken of this problem to anyone except your. . .your mother since you were born." Rance looked down at their entwined hands. "And now I've even betrayed that confidence," he added bitterly under his breath, his grip tightening painfully.

Hilda winced. "No. . .no, you haven't, not really," she whispered, swallowing painfully, and then managed to say in a stronger voice, "I was going to ask you if you knew what. . .and he was going to tell me anyway. Did. . .did he really say those exact words? That I'm. . .that I. . ." She couldn't voice the incredible, the unbelievable.

Rance looked at her steadily. "He didn't tell me very much. Just that you were not their natural daughter."

Hilda closed her eyes for a moment. Not their natural daughter!

"Your mother had always insisted there was no need to ever tell you that you'd been adopted," Rance continued in a low, compassionate voice. "Bob had wanted you to grow up with the knowledge, but she had. . .had an obsession that you would hate them. The older you grew, the more he was convinced she was wrong, but she. . . Apparently when she found out she had cancer, she made him promise never to tell you. And breaking that promise was what he wanted to talk about."

Hilda stared at him for a moment longer. He stared back at her steadily, and then she closed her eyes.

"So that's what it was," she said harshly at last. A shudder shook her body, and she pulled her hands away from his gentle grasp. "They should have told me," she said numbly. Then another emotion began to stir and strengthen. "Mum was right in a way. I think I do hate them. Not for adopting me, but. . .but. . . How dare they not tell me!" Her voice had gradually risen, and suddenly she sprang to her feet.

"Hildie, don't—"

She didn't hear the pleading in his voice. Rage drowned everything out. Rage against her mother. Rage against her father for leaving it too late to tell her. Rage against them both for dying. . .for leaving her alone. . .

"How could they not tell me! How could they! For over twenty years I've thought I was Hilda Garrett. But I'm not, am I? I'm not their daughter. They've lived a lie all these years! And if I'm not Hilda Garrett, who am I?"

She stumbled across to the side table and picked up a smiling family photo. Rance sprang to his feet, but he wasn't fast enough. It smashed in a tingle of glass against the nearest wall.

"Stop it, Hildie!" Rance roared.

Two strong hands descended violently on her shoulders, forcing her to stop as she blindly went for another photo. She fought against him for a moment, but he shook her, and then folded her tightly in his arms.

"Don't. . .don't. . ." he said over and over so brokenly that it penetrated the white heat raging through her, and her body at last went limp.

"They are your mother and father in every way that

really matters. Think about it. They made a mistake not telling you they adopted you. But they did love you! And no one can ever take that away from you," Rance insisted in a strong, passionate voice.

Then he pushed her far enough away from him to give her another shake, gentler this time, and to look her in the eye and glare fiercely at her. "And, oh, there've been times I've envied you," he added with fervent longing. "I've envied you having a father that loved you as much as Bob did, for having parents who gave you such a rich Christian heritage. And I've often longed that my father had loved my mother and been faithful to her even. . .even half as much. . ."

His voice faded, and he let her go slowly and stood very still for a moment. Then he added earnestly, sadly, "Watching Bob and listening to him taught me more about love and sacrifice and commitment than I ever dreamed possible. It made me realize how weak my own has been towards my parents, my. . .my Lord. . ."

Slow tears trickled down Hilda's face. "They should have told me," she whispered at last. She turned away from him.

"That's what I told your dad. He said he very nearly did just before you started school, but he didn't. He couldn't risk upsetting your mother." Rance hesitated, and then added firmly, "He also said that he rarely even thought about the fact that you weren't actually their flesh and blood. But after your mother died, he was worried in case something happened to him, too. But his promise to her worried him even more."

Hilda didn't move. After a few moments, she heard him move, and when she turned around he was carefully picking up pieces of glass from the floor. She hesitated and then stooped to pick up the shattered frame.

"I'm. . .I'm sorry," she whispered, staring down at the smiling, happy faces. "Please, don't. . .don't worry about the mess. I'll clear it up."

Rance straightened with shards of glass in his hand. "Hildie," he commenced, and then broke off. "I'd better get rid of these first," he muttered and strode from the room.

He was gone a few minutes. Hilda heard the rustle of paper and knew he was wrapping up the glass before discarding it in the garbage. When he returned, she was sitting down, still holding the photo, staring blankly into the distance.

"Rance," she began without moving, "surely their friends, like Marian Stevens, must have known I was adopted?"

Rance sat beside her again. "He said no one else knew besides him, your mother, and the authorities in Sydney who organized the adoption."

That startled her, and she looked at him wide eyed. "Sydney!"

He nodded abruptly. "One of the reasons he didn't—" He stopped and then said wearily, "Hildie, he did tell me a little more, but do you think we could have a cup of tea or something while we talk? I. . . I've had a rough few days, and I've just driven up from Sydney from—" He broke off abruptly, and dropped his eyes.

Despite her distress and bewilderment, something like relief stirred in Hilda. He had been away. He had not forgotten about her after all.

She stood up slowly and took a deep breath. "Yes, of course. Though I. . .I do want you to tell me everything you can remember he said," she warned him in a suddenly firm voice.

He raised his head, and a sudden glint of admiration

lightened his exhausted face. "There isn't really very much, but I will tell you all I know," he assured her without hesitation.

Between them they heated some soup, made some toast, set the table simply with some place mats, and sat down. Hilda automatically bowed her head and waited.

There was silence, and then Rance muttered, "You can say grace for us."

She glanced up at him quickly. His head was bowed and his eyes closed as he waited. She hesitated for a moment, and then prayed in a faltering voice, "O, Lord, we do thank You for. . .for all Your goodness and this food, and. . . ," she swallowed, and added earnestly, "and we do need Your strength, and Your help so much. Amen."

"Amen!" Rance's voice held a hint of desperation.

As they silently started to eat, Hilda looked across the table at him curiously. "How long were you waiting for me this evening?" she asked at last as the silence lengthened.

He hesitated and then smiled a little crookedly. "About an hour or so, I guess."

Her eyes widened. "Why on earth didn't you go over to the Stevens'?"

He looked down swiftly, and he hesitated before he said softly, "I was enjoying the peace and quiet here too much. There's something about the silent spaces that brings me closer to God. It helped," he added simply.

Then she remembered, and put down her own spoon. "Rance! You said something before about your world falling down around you? Has something else happened?"

He looked up at her briefly and then away again. "I don't want to talk about it," he grated out.

There was a great sadness in his eyes, and she remembered the night of the wedding rehearsal. She hesitated, and then fearing another rebuff, resumed trying to swallow food that could have been sawdust for all she tasted it. They ate in silence, and then Hilda made a pot of tea.

She couldn't quite bring herself to ask him more questions, even about what her father had said. "Rance, I'm so sorry about Maree," she said softly instead, as she handed him his steaming cup of tea.

He started, the tea slopping over the side of the cup. She bit her lip and waited, not sure what to do or say.

He was silent, looking down at the cup, running a long, lean finger along the edge of its saucer. "Thank you, Hildie, but I can't talk about it yet," he said at last very quietly and sadly, "especially at the moment."

As she took a sip of the fragrant beverage, Hilda silently watched him over the brim of her own cup. She suddenly remembered he had also said something about someone called Nathan and was about to ask him who he was, when Rance suddenly put down his own cup, took a deep breath, and said abruptly, "I promised to tell you what Bob said."

Hilda tensed.

"You know they were both in their late thirties before they married?" Rance began slowly. She nodded briefly, and he continued. "They very much wanted a child and were very disappointed for years."

Hilda nodded again. Tears blurred her eyes. "They often told me about those years," she said in a choked voice, and then added bitterly, "but they also said how delighted they were, but scared too, because she was well over forty when they found out she was pregnant. But that wasn't true, was it?"

"Yes, it was true," Rance said softly. She stared at him, and he continued hurriedly. "The baby died."

Rapidly he told her how, late in her pregnancy, they had received word of the death of Mavis Garrett's mother in Sydney. She had insisted on going down to the funeral, but while down there, she had slipped and broken her leg.

"Your father didn't say what happened any more than at the same time a baby girl was born prematurely and died a couple days later. They both took it very hard. It had been a difficult pregnancy from the start, and your mother apparently ended up on the verge of a breakdown."

Hilda gave a slight exclamation. "Dad told me once when she really went berserk at me in my teens that she'd once almost had a nervous breakdown," she said slowly.

Rance nodded. "I think it must have been touch and go, from what he said. She was still in hospital with her leg in traction when she overheard the staff talking about a baby who had been born the same day as their own baby and was up for adoption."

"Did. . .did he say anything about the. . .about my real mother?" Hilda whispered.

Rance shook his head gently. "No, he didn't. He told me that it became an obsession with Mavis to adopt you. It apparently took some time to persuade the powers that be."

"But they succeeded," Hilda said thoughtfully, "and I suppose they came home and never told anyone."

Rance hesitated, and then said slowly, "Your father didn't say, but it would seem so."

Hilda was silent, thinking back over the years. Now that she knew, it did explain a few times why her mother had been abrupt with her, even furiously angry, yelling, "How on earth do I know where you got your red hair from, but I'll have white hair if you don't stop asking such stupid questions!"

It explained so many other little things.

Rance's light touch on her hand brought her back to the present with a start. She looked at him inquiringly.

"I said I'll have to be going soon," he said softly, "My mother and step-father are expecting me tonight, and they'll be worried if I don't turn up soon. Will you be all right by yourself?"

"Oh," Hilda said blankly, suddenly remembering what he had said. "You've driven straight here from Sydney? No wonder you look so terrible!"

A rueful grin tilted his lips. "I look that bad, huh?"

No, you look like the nicest man I've ever met, suddenly flashed into Hilda's mind, astounding her. She frowned and said bluntly, "You do look absolutely exhausted. Are you sure you should drive anymore tonight? Your mother lives the other side of Dalby, doesn't she? Wouldn't you rather stay here?"

"Jean's gone home, hasn't she?"

She frowned slightly, "Yes, but that doesn't matter, does—oh!" She suddenly felt heat fill her face.

"Exactly," he said with his twisted smile. "Think what the neighbours would think! Or," he added shortly as he stood up, "more what some church people would think!"

As he drove off, Hilda was still wondering about the bitter tone in his voice when he had referred to the church people. And suddenly she was sorry that he had not offered to pray with her about all that they had talked about. It had been the kind of thing she knew he had often done with her father.

And it wasn't until she had re-entered the house that she remembered that she still didn't know who Nathan was, and that Rance had said something about "the world falling around you, too." Something more than the day's car trip from Sydney had happened to make him look so dreadful.

Suddenly Hilda wished quite desperately that she had insisted he stay despite any possible gossip. She had been so wrapped up in her own pain that she had been totally selfish of his own personal pain and needs.

Hilda slept little that night. For hours she lay awake going over every word Rance had said about her adoption. He had known so little. Why hadn't her real mother wanted her? Had she ever had another baby? Were there half-brothers and sisters somewhere?

And then the tears slid down her face because now she could never talk to her mother or father about it all, or rather, to the people she had always believed were her parents.

five

It was difficult to get an early start the next morning to take Polly to have her tests. But they made the appointment just in time, and Hilda left a forlorn collie to be ushered off by a nurse and drove to the other side of the city to the lookout at Picnic Point. It was a very popular tourist spot at the top of the cliffs looking down over the fertile Lockyer Valley stretching to the east.

She sat for a while in the sun gazing out across the tops of the giant old gum-trees. The sun glistened off matchbook-size vehicles on the highway that meandered its way down the mountain range. So many times over the years she had travelled on it, past the small villages scattered along the fertile valleys, the rich farm lands and the beautiful rolling hills that linked Toowoomba with the city of Brisbane almost one hundred miles away.

I wonder where my real mother grew up, Hilda thought. Was it in Sydney, or out in the country somewhere?

She jumped up restlessly and strode off along the paths that led to the large picnic areas looking down on the wide, flat, green surface of Tabletop Mountain a short distance away. The church youth group had organized a hike and spent the day climbing the relatively gentle slopes a few years before. Long before Rance had appeared on the scene.

Had her mother ever gone to church? Why had she given her baby away?

She deliberately tried to block off such thoughts and focus instead on Rance. During the long hours of the night, she had wondered again and again what was happening in his life. Why had he gone to Sydney? What on earth could that "immense problem" be that her father had mentioned?

A brisk wind sprang up and she shivered. She glanced at her watch. Still another few hours before she could pick up Polly. She had planned to do some shopping, but she wasn't in the mood now. Strolling over to the kiosk, she bought herself a hot drink and a meat pie. Reluctantly she returned to the shelter of the car.

As she ate her impromptu meal, it seemed strange sitting there by herself. It was the first time she had ever been to Picnic Point alone. Being mid-week, there were fewer people about. Suddenly she felt very lonely.

Something I'm going to have to get used to, she thought grimly. And although she managed to shrug off the gloomy thought, it returned with force as she later listened to the grave-faced vet.

"We'll have to wait for the biopsy result, but I'm pretty sure she has cancer," he told her directly.

A few days later, the diagnosis was confirmed, with the added news that it was considerably advanced and nothing could be done. Polly could live only a few weeks or months at the most. A course of cortisone tablets relieved any inflammation, as the vet had explained, and the beautiful creature started to brighten up, but Hilda knew it wouldn't last.

Hilda's heart was very sore. Over the years, she had shown the collie at various dog exhibitions and won several awards. It had been a dream of her's to one day start breeding and selling collies. Now, that could never be with Polly.

Hilda let Polly sleep inside the house, but the farmhouse was still often far too empty and lonely at the end of a day

on the tractor. The preparation of the paddocks for planting wheat and barley had been finished, but there were still
a few acres of sorghum stubble to plow in that her father
had decided to keep fallow.

Several times in the lonely evenings she wished she could
contact Rance. But the phone was never answered at the
manse, and she had no idea how to contact his mother.

The days dragged by. Marian Stevens rang regularly and
insisted she come to them for meals. Other folk from church
also checked on how she was, but she gently refused most
offers of help and hospitality. With Marian she could shed
a few tears as they talked about her parents. That initial
sharp pain of grief and loss gradually faded to a dull ache.

Then one day sometime after Rance's visit, Hilda asked
Marian if she had known about her adoption. The shocked
expression on the older woman's face told Hilda the answer. After asking Marian not to mention it to anyone,
Hilda poured it all out to her wide-eyed friend.

"I remember vividly the day they brought you home,"
Marian said thoughtfully after a while. "Mavis had been
in hospital quite a long time after you had been born prematurely." She stopped awkwardly, and then continued
hastily. "You were a beautiful, auburn-haired mite, full of
smiles. They were so very proud of you."

"Do you by any chance know which hospital I was born
in, Aunt Marian?" Hilda asked wistfully.

Marian Stevens looked at her sharply. "Yes, as a matter
of fact, I do," she said slowly. "Mavis insisted on going to
the hospital she'd heard so much about over the years from
Jean Drew and myself. That's where I met Jean. I didn't
finish my nurse's training, but Jean did and stayed on there
as a sister. She's always been very proud of the place's
reputation. But unfortunately, she wasn't there at the time.

In fact she had been overseas for a year or more doing more training or something. It was about then I lost track of Jean, for some years in fact. Anyway, the hospital was also in a suburb where Mavis had an aunt that Bob could stay with."

"Aunt Lily," murmured Hilda. "And the name of the hospital?"

Marian told her, and then hesitated as though about to say something else. Hilda rushed in, changing the subject, and it was obvious that Marian followed her lead reluctantly.

So, at least I know where I was born, Hilda thought wistfully as she drove home later that night.

The evening that the last paddock was ploughed for the time being, Hilda wearily trudged up to the house feeling depressed, filthy dirty, and thoroughly exhausted. Would she be able to keep on running the farm like this? At least there had been no mechanical breakdowns. That would have been something well out of her expertise, and very costly to have done. As the days had passed she realized more and more how much work her father had done despite her increasing help the last couple of years.

Sadly she had to face the fact that she had to make a big decision about whether she could keep the farm or not. There wasn't enough money to really employ someone full time, probably not even part time, she thought a little bitterly. Even if the Lord gave her a bumper crop, there was no guarantee the Wheat Board would be able to find enough markets for it and the huge harvests from all the other hopeful, desperate farmers like herself.

She soaked for a long time in a luxurious full bath, despite the fact that the rain water tanks needed a few storms to fill them. She was leisurely dressing in a comfortable pair of jeans and blouse when the phone rang. Expecting to hear Marian's cheerful voice, something leaped inside her when long distance pips sounded, and it was Rance.

"Oh, Rance, I'm so glad you rang. I've been wanting to discuss something with you," she started eagerly.

There was silence for a moment, and then he said a little huskily, "I should have rung you before I came back down here to Sydney. I'm sorry, there's been a lot to sort out, and Nathan's also been sick. He's had a bout of bronchitis and asthma, but he's well on the mend now." He paused again, and then asked in a firmer voice, "How have you been?"

Hilda closed her eyes. Nathan again. Suddenly she longed quite desperately to see him. "Polly's got cancer in the nose," she blurted out.

"Hildie, no!"

"The. . .the vet says he doesn't know how long. Cortisone helped at first, but now. . ." Her voice choked.

He asked her a few more questions and then, "Is that what you wanted to talk to me about, Hildie?" he asked quietly, after another pause.

Tears stung her eyes again, so glad there was one person who still called her that. Had her father ever told him how much she had always hated her name?

"I. . .yes. . .I mean, no," Hilda said at last.

She there and then made up her mind about something that she had been contemplating ever since his last visit.

She straightened, and tilted her chin. "I've decided," she began in as firm a voice as she could manage, "I've decided to try and find out who my biological parents are."

Rance was silent for a long moment. "I'm not too sure it's always a good idea to dig into the past, Hildie," he said slowly, and then added briskly, "I'll be home as soon as I can. We'll talk about it first. See you then," and hung up.

Hilda replaced the phone reluctantly. She frowned. What was there to talk about? After all, it was her decision alone to make.

"Have you really thought and prayed this right through?" a grave-faced Rance asked a defiant Hilda a few days later.

She looked back at him steadily. "I don't think I can honestly say I'm sure I know exactly what God wants me to do, but surely it can't be wrong just finding out who my mother was?"

"It depends what your motives are for finding out."

She looked away. What were her motives? Were they as simple as she thought? "Isn't just wanting to know who I am enough motive?" she snapped at last.

"No, I don't believe it is," he answered quietly. "Have you any idea what you'll do with the knowledge? Its effects on you and your biological parents must be considered."

They were sitting in a sunny, sheltered spot on the verandah, looking out across the dark paddocks that stretched far into the distance. The setting sun was turning a few clouds low on the horizon a golden delight. A drop in temperature the past few days had caused the winter slacks and jumpers to be hauled out of cupboards as the flat black soil plains braced itself for a cold winter.

Hilda shivered, and stood up. "It's too cold out here. Let's go into the lounge room," she muttered.

She busied herself shutting doors and checking that windows were closed before she turned on the reverse cycle air-conditioner. Soon its warmth started taking away the chill air in the room.

As she sat across from Rance, she observed as casually as she could, "Feels like winter may start early this year. I wish it would rain so we can get the wheat well up before any heavy frosts."

Rance remained silent, frowning down at his hands.

"I have to know who I am, Rance," she burst out. "It's as though suddenly I don't have any identity, any roots."

His gaze darkened as he looked at her. "When your parents adopted you, they not only gave you their name, but their roots as well."

"Oh, Rance, don't. . .please don't get me wrong! I've been one of the most fortunate people to have been given such a heritage, but I. . .I still need to know." Tears filled her eyes as she said rapidly, "I don't even know where my red hair and blue eyes come from. That was always one thing I used to pester Mum and Dad about when I was little, and the kids at school called me names. They always just said they didn't know, and that I was their very own, beautiful copper-headed princess.

"And there's my name. I've always hated it," she added with a touch of bitterness. "Is it the name my real mother gave me, and if so, why? It's such an old fashioned name, and I've always wondered why on earth I was called that. There were never any relatives in Mum or Dad's families called 'Hilda.' And. . .and it was one of the times Mum yelled at me when I kept pestering her about it. She went right off her head." She sniffed back a tear, and said forlornly, "I don't even have any close relatives now. What if there are grandparents somewhere, brothers, sisters?"

"But that's what I was just trying to say, Hildie love." Rance's voice was gentle and kind, his face filled with compassion. "Will you want to meet them? Will they want to have any contact with you? What if there's a veto on any contact?"

"A veto?"

He studied her large eyes for a moment, and then sighed. "Do you know anything about the adoption laws at all?"

"I know that a bill was passed allowing people to find out who their biological parents are, but I don't even know where to start," she admitted. "The. . .the only thing in our area phone directory was some adoption support group with a Brisbane number."

"Yes, I know there are such groups," Rance said slowly. "There are also groups that can act as mediators, but there are also Adoption Privacy groups that are opposed to the new laws. Some people are afraid of their privacy being invaded. There've been some sad cases where adopted children have turned up out of the blue and caused tremendous problems. And then mothers have tracked down a child. Imagine how more shocked you would have been if your natural mother had suddenly arrived claiming to be your real mother before you even knew you were adopted! Parents or children can lodge their names on a contact veto register, but there have still been problems where people have made contact illegally."

There was silence. "I wouldn't want to upset anyone," Hilda said at last in a small voice.

A skeptical look passed across Rance's face. Hilda suddenly remembered her lie to Gail about being engaged to Jim, and went scarlet.

"I. . .it's because I did cause so much hurt then, to Gail and Jim, as well as Dad and myself that I couldn't. . .I wouldn't . . .," she blurted out in a stifled voice. Then she straightened, and looked at him steadily. "I've apologized to Gail for that lie, and I've asked God to forgive me too. I know they've both forgiven me and that's all in the past now."

Rance's expression softened again. "I"m sorry, Hildie. I

wasn't referring to your past mistakes." He gave a sudden self-derisive snort. "I'm the last person to bring up someone's past! And I've seen a big change in Hilda Garrett since last year. You're a very beautiful woman, and I don't just mean on the outside."

Hilda gaped at him. He actually thought she was beautiful!

Something flickered deep inside Hilda. She wasn't sure what the feeling was, except she suddenly had an overwhelming desire that this man continue to think well of her.

My goodness, he's a wonderful man, she thought fervently. *If he were my fiancé, there would be no way I could ever give him up.*

Rance's expression changed again. Hilda suddenly realized their eyes were clinging, searching. There was something in his dark eyes she couldn't interpret. . .a heat. . .

Something melted inside her. She started to lean toward him. Then she gave a little gasp, and sprang to her feet. For a moment she had quite desperately wanted him to kiss her.

Rance stood up also. "I've got to go," he said shortly.

Hilda could feel the warmth in her face, and not for the first time wished her fair skin did not flush so easily. Trying to speak naturally, she said, "I was hoping you might be able to help me, Rance. I don't really know where to start. And. . .and I wanted to ask you who this Nathan is you've been so concerned about."

"You mean the grapevine that exists in our church in Toowoomba hasn't done its job out here?" Anger and pain filled Rance's face. He hesitated and then straightened his shoulders as though bracing himself. "Nathan is my nine-year-old son. I only found out he existed last year."

Speechless, Hilda felt her mouth drop as she stared at him.

"I thought your father had told you about him. You seemed to know about Maree breaking our engagement," Rance said slowly, the expression on his face changing.

With considerable difficulty Hilda found her voice. "Dad . . .Dad only told me about Maree, and on the way to the reception briefly mentioned that you had an immense problem. At the same time he said he had decided to tell me. . . tell me what I now know must have been about my adoption," she finished a little breathlessly.

"I don't know what I would have done if I hadn't had Bob to talk to about the whole sorry mess," Rance said softly. "He was more like a father to me than my own has ever been." He suddenly ran a hand through his hair as Hilda felt the still-too-ready tears gathering behind her eyes. "Perhaps it was so easy for him to be so non-judgmental and understanding of what I was going through because of his own past." A slight smile twisted his lips. "Looks like you and I both have yesterdays we have to sort out so we can cope with what God wants us to do today and tomorrow."

Before she could speak, he suddenly moved briskly towards the door. "I've just got to go. Afraid I can't go into more details about my past now," he added abruptly. "I'll tell you more some other time, if. . .if you're still interested."

Rance paused and turned back to her. He must have mistaken the disappointed look he saw on her face, and said firmly, "I'm sorry, Hildie. There's still so much to sort out about Nathan and a job for me, that I'm afraid I just haven't got the time to help you as I'd like to at the moment. Perhaps you can start by ringing that adoption group in Brisbane. I'm sure they can tell you more about what you have to do. If not, there are various government community and family departments that could help you."

He left rather abruptly, almost as though he were scared to get involved anymore with her, Hilda thought a little resentfully. He seemed to take it for granted she wasn't interested in his affairs. She scowled as his car disappeared down the long, bumpy track to the main road. How could he know she was becoming more and more vitally interested in everything that concerned Rance Telford?

There had suddenly been so many, many things she wanted to talk about with him. She longed to know more about Nathan. Nine years ago Rance would have been at university. And that was around the time he had been converted. And all this time since he had become a Christian and trained and been in the ministry, there had been a son he had known nothing about? But how come he'd found out now?

He had actually said she was beautiful. As she went back inside, a warm glow spread through her. It chased away some of her disappointment that he had not wanted to spend more time with her. And it was nice that he had been concerned enough about her to travel all this way to see her. She wondered if he had known that she had suddenly longed for him to kiss her. Perhaps that was why he had rushed off the way he had, she thought with dismay, and a sudden feeling of desolation.

He'd said nothing about where he was staying. Marian Stevens had told her he had resigned from the ministry in Toowoomba, which had explained the desolate air of the manse and his looking for a job. Her expression cleared a little. Perhaps he was still with his mother and step-father near Dalby. And then she scowled again. She still didn't know where she could ring him.

It wasn't until she was tossing and turning unable to sleep late that night, that she faced up to her increasing sense of loss that he had not kissed her. She sat up abruptly in bed.

You stupid idiot! You're coming close to falling in love with the man! she berated herself. *The man has just become an instant father. The last thing he needs is to have to fend off a woman who thinks she falling for him!*

Suddenly she found herself praying. "Oh, God," she pleaded foolishly, "don't let me like him too much." After a moment or two she calmed down, and then added beseechingly, "Please guard and keep us both. Show us what You want us to do."

She started to tremble as she tried to relax on the bed again. Suddenly she was scared—scared that it was too late. She had a sneaking suspicion she had already gone past liking to loving Rance Telford.

"If this is all part of Your will, please take away the fear and give me Your courage," she whispered at last.

Hilda rang the adoption support group in Brisbane the next morning. The woman who answered was very kind and helpful, although she too tried to warn her of some of the difficulties that finding her mother might create. To set the ball in motion, all Hilda had to do was apply for her original birth certificate. When she had been adopted, the Garretts would have filled out information for an amended birth certificate. To obtain the original she had to provide adequate proof of her identity.

She was sitting staring at the notes she had made as the woman talked, when the phone rang. It was Rance, and the sudden peculiar gymnastics of her heart shook her.

"I just rang the local Social Security office," he started briskly. "They said your parents would have had legal papers about your adoption. Even if those had not disappeared, you would still have to apply for your original birth certificate. You just need adequate proof of your identity."

"I. . .I know," she said in a husky voice, trying to pull herself together. "I've just rung that support group in Brisbane."

"Good," Rance said rather abruptly. There was a pause, and then he added a little more gently, "So, are you going to go ahead with it all?"

"Yes, I am," she said as firmly as she was capable of at that moment.

"Well, if there's anything I can do to help, I want you to know I really want to."

Hilda wondered why his voice had suddenly gone so deep and husky. She hesitated and then said quite sharply, "Well then, I should at least know where you're living now or have your phone number so I can reach you."

"Oh, I thought I told you I was staying with my mother. Bob had the number," he said with surprise in his voice.

"He probably did," she snapped through suddenly gritted teeth, "but I don't know your step-father's name!"

"You don't?" He told her the name in a voice still full of surprise.

Hilda was struck dumb for a few moments, then she said in a strangled voice, "That man's your step-father!"

The man was a well-known grazier and farmer, who also happened to be very wealthy and influential!

There was amused understanding in Rance's voice. "He certainly is!" Before she could say anything more, he said good-bye briskly and hung up.

Hilda was intrigued. She knew even less about their former minister than she had thought. And how had the step-son of such a prominent man come to enter the ministry of the church?

Well, it was none of her business, her sensible side tried to tell her. That other side of her she had discovered during the dark hours of the night wanted desperately to know all there was to know about this man who was becoming more and more important to her.

six

"No, I'm sorry, Lawrence isn't here at the moment. Who did you say was calling?"

Lawrence? Hilda bit her lip. She was bitterly disappointed that he was not home to share her news. Hilda gave her name again in a stifled voice.

The woman's voice at the other end of the phone became even more reserved as she said in a cold voice, "Oh, yes, Miss Garrett, my son has mentioned you. I'll tell him you called," and then hung up.

So that was Rance's mother. And now Hilda knew how Rance had come by his unusual name. It was merely an abbreviation of "Lawrence." Hilda replaced the phone receiver reluctantly.

She sighed as she glanced down at the birth certificate clutched in her hand. There had been several more calls from Rance, but it had been the first time she had yielded to her desire to ring him. He had usually sounded tired and discouraged, but, to her frustration and disappointment, steadfastly refused to talk about his problems. He always enquired after Polly and wanted to know about Hilda's search for her mother. So when he had not rung for a few evenings, she had not been able to resist the urgent need to tell him her exciting news. Much good it had done her, and for some reason, his mother had disapproved of her trying to contact him.

Hilda reached out to pick up the phone and ring the Stevenses. Then she hesitated and changed her mind. Jim and Gail had been back from their delayed honeymoon trip for some time now, but she knew they were very busy finishing off some plowing delayed by their wedding. Besides, she had pledged Mrs. Stevens to secrecy about her adoption and never even mentioned to her the decision to find her natural mother.

Hilda spread out the certificate again with a trembling hand. There it was in black and white. She had been named Hilda Louise. The woman who had given birth to her was a Margaret Louise Jones, and the line opposite "Father" said simply "Unknown." The address given for her mother was at a place called Paddington, an inner suburb of Sydney.

A great longing filled Hilda to pack her bag and get to Sydney as fast as she could. There was always a slim chance Margaret Louise Jones still lived at that address, or perhaps someone there or in the neighbourhood would remember a pregnant woman. She caught her breath. Jones was a very common name. Had her mother given her real name and address?

But Hilda knew she couldn't leave Polly. The dog had been gradually getting weaker. She had started to refuse all food, even the special delicacies she had always loved. All she was taking was fluids.

And then, it was very likely the wheat would have to be planted any day now. Several evenings the storm clouds had rolled over without fulfilling their promise of rain. Once the ground had been soaked enough to give a reasonably moist sub-soil, it would only take a few days to dry out enough for the tractor to be started again.

Hilda had very reluctantly approached a real estate agent to come and give her an estimate of what the place was worth. She was still trying to decide what to do, but even if she put the farm on the market, the next crop would have to be planted.

The phone trilled its urgent summons right beside her, and Hilda jumped.

"It's Jim here, Hilda. Could Gail and I come over and see you for awhile? We've got a proposition to put to you."

It was Friday. Hilda had been dreading another long evening by herself and eagerly agreed.

Jim and Gail had already been over a few times since their return, and to her own private surprise, she and Gail were well on the way to becoming good friends. The fact that they had both suffered tragedy in their lives had somehow drawn them closer together. Hilda also knew it was because she herself was letting God change her so much from the selfish girl who had always been trying to impress Jim and his mother with her abilities.

So when the headlights neared the house a few minutes later, Hilda went out eagerly to welcome them. But it wasn't Jim's Holden after all. Rance's lithe figure stepped from the car and strode along the lighted path toward her.

"Oh, Rance! What a gorgeous surprise," she called out, and impulsively rushed down the steps towards him. "I just tried to ring you!"

Her eyes were fixed on his gentle smile. In her haste she had forgotten her feet were bare and stubbed her toe on a cracked, uneven piece of the path.

"Whoa, there," Rance's amused voice exclaimed.

As she gave an exclamation of pain and stumbled, he grabbed her. It seemed the most natural thing in the world to feel his arms close around her and to raise her face for his kiss. His arms tightened convulsively, and then their lips met. Hilda felt a surge of heat and the delightful feeling that this was where she belonged, in this man's arms.

She only came back to earth when she heard Rance give a muffled groan and suddenly wrench his lips from hers.

"Hildie!" he gasped in a breathless, appalled voice. "I'm so sorry, I don't know why. . ." His dazed voice broke off.

There was a crunch of gravel, and they both turned as they became aware of the sound of a car rolling to a stop. They stood frozen for a moment as the head lights surrounded them. Hilda suddenly realized Rance's warm arms were still holding her close and pushed him away.

"It's Jim," she said breathlessly.

Rance stiffened, and she saw him swallow as he took a step back from her.

"Gail's with him," she added defensively, hurt stinging her suddenly. "Jim just rang and said they wanted to talk to me about something."

Jim and Gail called out their greetings. As she heard the amused speculation in their voices, Hilda knew she must be crimson with embarrassment. She quickly ushered them all inside, and the awkward moment soon passed. Gail had brought over a delicious chocolate caramel slice which she claimed was a new recipe she had tried. Soon they were relaxing with hot drinks.

"Not bad, not bad at all for a beginner cook," Jim teased Gail gently. At Hilda's raised eyebrow, Jim laughed. "Mum apparently had to teach Sister Brandon how to cook when she came to housekeep for us. They managed very successfully to keep it a secret from her boss!"

Hilda grinned at them both. When she glanced across at Rance, he was watching her with an indecipherable expression. She sobered quickly, and then felt relieved when his eyes suddenly lit up with his old sweet smile.

"Hildie's an excellent cook," he murmured softly.

She felt the pink rising in her cheeks and looked hastily

away, still feeling confused by their encounter outside. "You said you had a proposition to put to me, Jim," she said hurriedly.

Jim hesitated and looked across at Gail. "It was Gail's idea really. You tell her, sweetheart."

A few minutes later, Hilda was staring at them wide eyed. "You want to share farm this property?" she gasped, excitement clutching at her.

"I've got some capital from my father's estate that I've been wondering what to do with," Gail said quickly. "Jim heard yesterday that you were considering selling. There isn't enough money to buy you out yet, but there is enough to hire some workman and to come to some arrangement with you about using your machinery and everything. Jim's quite sure he could run the two farms as one, especially with some capital to start off with. You could still live in the house, or rent it out, but that would be entirely up to you. Of course, it all depends on whether or not you need the money from an immediate sale. We would like to have first option on it in the future if you want to sell in a few years. But Jim thought—"

"Oh, no!" Hilda said passionately. "The last thing I want to do is to sell the farm that Dad's family has owned for so long. But I didn't know what else to do. It. . .I. . ." She burst into tears of sheer relief. "Its. . .a. . .simply. . .wonderful. . .idea," she gasped between sobs.

It was Rance who reached her before Jim.

Neither noticed the delighted glance Jim and Gail gave each other as their ex-minister held Hilda tightly, murmuring soothing words until she had forced back the tears of relief and happiness.

She was still clinging to Rance's hands with both of hers, when she at last looked across at Gail and Jim with a rather damp smile. "I knew God would have a plan for me. And now it seems as though He's opening the way for me to go and find—"

She broke off, remembering that Gail and Jim knew nothing of her adoption. She hesitated for a moment, and glanced up at Rance. He started to withdraw his hands, and only then did she realize she was nestling into his side as though it was a perfectly natural place to be.

She sat up hastily, beginning to blush furiously. "I seem to be making a habit of crying all over you, Rance," she said with considerable confusion.

"Don't mind in the least," he said cheerfully and grinned at her, "especially when it's because you're happy about something for a change."

Hilda found herself pulling a face at him. A rush of embarrassment and nerves suddenly filled her. She turned quickly away from the sudden gleam in his eyes back to Jim and Gail.

They eagerly began to pour out the ideas they'd already come up with. Despite Hilda's protests, Jim insisted that they must get their solicitors to draw up a legal contract for them to sign. Rance showed his involvement and interest in Hilda's affairs by making a couple of wise suggestions, proving to Hilda that he was more familiar with the working of a farm than she had expected.

"Well, that's about all we can do until the legal boys get together," Jim said at last with considerable satisfaction as he surveyed the notes he had ended up jotting down. He closed the notebook with a snap and looked across at Rance. "And we still haven't asked Rance what he's doing with himself. We were very sorry to hear the church in Toowoomba voted not to continue to employ you, mate," he added gravely. "We're going to miss you very much."

Rance's face was suddenly grim. "Yes, I was very disappointed by their attitude," he said abruptly. He looked across at Hilda's shocked face. "Didn't you know I got the sack?"

"Aunt Marian just said you'd resigned!" she exclaimed in dismay.

"Oh, I resigned all right. But no minister could stay after being so roundly condemned for having a child out of wedlock. It didn't seem to matter to the majority of them that it was something that had happened in my life before Christ saved me and showed me how to live His way!"

Hilda was even more shocked by the bitterness and anger in him. She stared at him speechlessly.

"I actually stopped by here tonight on my way through to Toowoomba to stay the night there," Rance continued curtly. "I'm moving to Sydney for the foreseeable future, and it'll give me an earlier start for the trip. The church's ministerial placement board thinks there may be a church down there who'll contact me about a ministry with them."

A cold hand clutched at Hilda's heart as she stared at Rance. Jim said something about being sorry to hear that, and then Hilda found her breath.

"Your mother didn't say anything about you leaving when I rang you this evening," Hilda said in a strangled voice.

A shadow crossed his face. "That's right, you did say something when I first arrived about trying to ring me, didn't you? I'm afraid my mother isn't a Christian and was very disappointed when I went into the ministry. Now she's very angry and upset by everything. What did you want me for, Hilda?"

I want you to stay. I want you to help me. I want to help you overcome all the pain in you. I want you to need me as much as I need you, trembled on her lips.

Instead, she heard herself blurt out wildly, "I had news about my search, and. . .and wanted to know what was happening about Nathan."

"It's obvious that you two have a few things to talk about," Jim chipped in hastily. He stood up. Then he glanced at his watch and frowned. "Have you booked into a motel, Rance?" When Rance shook his head, he said urgently, "Look, it's going to be very late now by the time you get to Toowoomba. Most accommodations will likely be booked out. Why don't you come over after you finish talking to Hilda and stay the night with us instead?"

Hilda looked pleadingly at Rance as he started to refuse and was very relieved when he suddenly changed his mind and said simply, "Thanks a lot, Jim."

Rance accompanied Hilda outside to wave off the young couple. "I'm so glad about the farm, Hildie," he said quietly into the darkness after they had gone.

Hilda tucked her arm inside his elbow without thinking, her mind still on all the things they had thrashed out with Jim and Gail. "So am I," she said fervently. The strong body beside her tensed. She quickly withdrew her hand and turned back to the house. "I received my original birth certificate today," she blurted out. Her voice was unnaturally bright even to her own ears. She bit her lip.

Rance drew in a deep breath, but he was silent until she had led the way back inside and handed him the certificate. "So your name has always been Hilda," he mused softly. "What about Louise?"

Hilda folded her arms over each other as a tremor passed through her. "No, it's Mavis," she said abruptly, and as he looked up at her, she added with a nervous smile, "I think I was hoping it wouldn't be Hilda. I've always hated it."

A surprised look crossed his face. "Why? I've always

thought it a unique name."

"Hmmph," she snorted, "that almost describes it, but I think the right word should be antique!"

A strange expression crossed Rance's face. He turned quickly away, but she thought he murmured, "unique. There's certainly only one Hildie."

She didn't know for a moment whether it was a compliment or not. *Probably not,* she thought sourly. *Not with my past performance.*

"Where's Polly?" Rance asked suddenly.

"She spends all day in here now, and the nights out in the laundry. She. . .she's stopped eating these last few days, but she's still drinking," Hilda said sadly.

She thought for a moment Rance started to move toward her, but he stilled and then went toward the back door. She followed him slowly. He was crouched beside Polly when she arrived in the laundry doorway. Polly sat up slowly, and wagged her tail at them both, then she walked stiffly over to the water dish and drank thirstily.

There was nothing to do or say except to pat her gently until the beautiful dog settled down again with her head on her paws. Her once beautiful coat of hair was no longer glossy, and her ears drooped.

They turned off the light again and returned silently to the kitchen. Hilda gave a quivering sigh. "It's going to be very lonely here without her," she murmured huskily, "and you're not going to be around either, Rance. Are. . .are you really moving to Sydney permanently?"

He ran his hand through his ruffled hair. "That's where Nathan is," he said evenly. His face tightened. "I've been desperately wanting him to come and live with me, but they. . .he. . . Oh, Hildie, it's a dreadful mess!"

"Would. . .would you like to tell me about it?" she asked

hesitantly.

He searched her face, and for one tingling moment she thought he would lower his guard and talk about it all to her. But he said quickly "You've got enough problems of your own." He looked down at the birth certificate. "Are you going to continue trying to find your biological mother?"

Hilda swallowed her disappointment. "Yes, I want to— need to—very much." Her face lit up. "And sooner than I thought possible because of Jim and Gail taking over the working of the farm."

"I do hope you don't get hurt, Hildie."

"That's a risk I'm afraid I have to take," she said a little mistily. "Do you know where you'll be living in Sydney?"

His face closed up again. "Friends of mine from my theological training days have offered to let me stay until I can get a flat or house to rent."

His expression was so forbidding, Hilda dared not ask him if he would keep in touch. Instead, she said earnestly, "You've been so good to me Rance, and Dad thought of you very highly. If. . .if there's ever anything I can do to help you, will you let me know?" she finished in a rush as she saw him start to scowl.

"I'm not sure if that would be wise, Hildie," he said very softly after a brief pause. He straightened and added decisively, "I'd better go, or I'll be keeping the Stevenses out of bed too late."

Rance strode outside, and Hildie trailed miserably after him, wondering what he meant. At the top of the steps, he turned. When she reached him, they stared at each other silently. Then she saw him swallow convulsively. As though he could not help himself, he reached out his hand and slid a gentle finger down her soft cheek, leaving a trail of fire that ignited Hilda's senses.

As she drew in a sharp breath, he said very quietly, "Don't come down to the car with me."

She stood frozen, frantically trying to think of something to say that would stop him leaving like this.

He whispered, "Bye, Hildie love," and turned and disappeared into the blackness of the night.

Hilda spent a long, restless night. Surely that had not been a final good-bye? Surely Rance would contact her when he settled down permanently? It took a long time before she was able to commit her confusion and uncertainty to the Lord and fall into a sound asleep.

Polly's whimpering brought her wide awake not long after dawn. Shrugging on her warm bathrobe she raced out to the laundry. As she saw her, Polly cried out even more pitifully, trying desperately, and unsuccessfully, to get up on her back legs.

"Oh, Polly dear. Oh, Polly you poor darling. What is it?"

But the answer was obvious. Although Hilda tried hard to soothe her, the dog became more distressed, and kept trying to struggle to her feet the moment Hilda made a move to go and phone the vet. Then she would rest for a moment, panting rapidly, and then the dreadful crying and struggling commenced again.

At last Hilda had to leave her, and as she stumbled back inside to the phone, the crying and whimpering increased in volume. The receiver was in her shaking hand when she paused and listened intently. Yes, it was a car approaching.

"Oh, thank You, Lord," she said tearfully as she raced outside.

It was Rance.

Hilda was in the driveway as the car stopped with a jolt and Rance flung open the car. "Hildie! What the—"

"Oh, Rance, Rance! Its Polly. . . ," she cried desperately as he grabbed her by the arms.

Together they raced back to Polly. The collie subsided weakly as they crouched beside her.

"I. . .I was just going to ring the vet's emergency number to tell them I was bringing her straight in," Hilda said softly, fighting back the tears as she once again stopped Polly's pathetic struggle to try and get up.

Rance placed a gentle arm around her shoulders. "Hildie, you do know what they have to do," he asked hesitantly.

She swallowed and said as calmly as she could, "Yes, of course."

"You stay with her, and I'll ring them. Is the number near the phone?"

She nodded briefly. His hand tightened for a moment, and then he disappeared. When he returned he said briskly, "I'll stay with her until you get changed. They'll meet us at the surgery."

"Us? But you. . ."

"Go on, love," he said so tenderly, she smiled blindly at him through her tear-filled eyes and did as he said.

It was a harrowing trip into Toowoomba with Hilda holding Polly as best she could, but on the silent trip home later that morning the car seemed sadly empty and Hilda's heart ached. She shed a few silent tears, but most of her tears for Polly had fallen as she had watched her weaken over the weeks.

As the car turned into the farm driveway Hilda burst out with, "I. . .I don't know what I'm going to do without you to be there when I need you, Rance."

"God will use someone else, of course, Hildie," Rance

said in such a harsh voice, that Hilda couldn't say another word.

She opened her door as soon as the car stopped, but Rance gave a sudden slight groan and gripped her arm tightly. "Oh, Hildie, sweetheart, I'm sorry. I don't know just why I turned into your driveway on an impulse at the last moment this morning. I certainly hadn't planned to, but I haven't been able to get the hurt look in your eyes last night out of my mind."

A firm hand touched her chin and turned her averted face toward him. "And now I've hurt you again. I should let you disappear out of my life for your sake, but I'm not strong enough, I'm afraid. Would. . .would it be okay if I rang you sometimes?"

She searched his eyes. Regret, confusion, and a hint of desperation stared back at her. Somewhere she drummed up the courage to put into words the wish that had come to her sometime during the long hours of the night.

"If you really mean that," she began slowly, watching him carefully for his reaction, "then do you think there's any possibility I could hitch a lift with you to Sydney?"

She thought she saw something like hope flash briefly into his eyes, and then knew she must have been mistaken. His lips tightened and her heart sank. She looked swiftly away.

Rance let go of her and sat back. "To search for Margaret Louise?"

There was a fraction of a pause and then Hilda nodded. She wasn't ready to admit that perhaps that was no longer her primary reason.

"Have you somewhere to stay?"

Hilda nodded again. "Jean Drew said anytime."

She dared to glance at him again. Suddenly he shrugged,

and grinned his little lopsided smile at her. Her heart leaped.

"Think you could be ready in half an hour?"

Relief swept through her on a surging tide. "You're on!" she beamed at him.

seven

It was closer to an hour than thirty minutes by the time Hilda had thrown a few belongings together and made phone calls to the Stevenses and Jean Drew. Jim assured her he would organize planting her wheat if she had not returned in time. But, as they started off, it was the knowing amusement in Jim's voice that caused her to feel constrained and uneasy with Rance.

He picked up on her discomfort, and any conversation was kept to general topics and the surrounding scenery, anything but their own private lives. Because of her disturbed night and the trauma of saying good-bye to Polly, Hilda dozed off and on for the first few hours. Then she insisted on driving while Rance had a rest. They stopped to stretch their legs a couple of times and fill up the petrol tank. It wasn't until they stopped for a longer break at McDonalds in the city of Tamworth that the atmosphere between them eased.

Tamworth hosted the huge Australian Country Music Festival every January, and they were soon into a lively discussion of the merits of country western music. Hilda was delighted to find he shared her wide ranging taste in music.

Hilda thoroughly enjoyed the next part of the trip southeast down the range at Murrurundi and the beautiful rolling hills of the Hunter Valley. It had been dark for some time, and they were both weary by the time they reached the F3 Freeway between Newcastle and Sydney. They had continued to share the driving, but Hilda was only too happy for Rance to drive the last stretch.

Once on the freeway, Hilda had expected not to stop again until they at least reached the Normanhurst area, one of the northern suburbs of Sydney where Rance's friends lived. But they had been on the freeway for some-time when Rance slowed and took the exit to a brightly lit, huge service center.

Hilda had been enjoying the comfortable silence and the smooth, fast travel on the freeway. She yawned and stretched. "Getting too tired, Rance?" she asked sympathetically. "Would you like me to drive again after all?"

"Nope," he said in the quiet voice she enjoyed so much, "I've decided we'll be arriving too late to expect David and Kim to get us an evening meal, and I'm starving."

She laughed. "That Big Mac does seem a long time ago. But this complex wasn't here the last trip Dad and I took to Sydney."

She was looking around her with interest at the large number of petrol and diesel pumps and the dozen or more big transport vehicles. As he drove slowly over to the restaurant parking area, Hilda did not notice the quick glance Rance directed at her. It was the first time he had heard her so easily mention her father.

When Hilda returned from the rest room to the dining area, she saw Rance just hanging up the public phone. She looked at his smiling face inquiringly.

"Well, that's settled. Kim's quite happy for you to stay the night with them."

She opened her mouth to protest at his high-handed organizing on her behalf and paused as she saw the fatigue in his face. She suddenly realized that Jean lived at least another half-hour from his friends' place, and he would have had to drive her there and return.

"Oh, I'm sorry, Rance. I didn't think what a nuisance I'd be."

His smile was the very gentle, beautiful one that so transformed his face. It seemed like forever since she had last seen it. As he touched her elbow and started propelling her into the restaurant, she caught her breath. Heat radiated along her arm.

"Never a nuisance, Hildie. I've really enjoyed your company. The last trip down here was long and lonely."

Hilda waited until they had started eating their delicious meal before she ventured to say, "Rance, that last trip to Sydney you mentioned, was. . .was that just after Dad's funeral?"

Rance paused with food halfway to his mouth and looked across the table at her. He put down his fork. "No, I flew down that time, late on Tuesday. I had intended to drive down on Easter Monday."

She stared at him. All that he had done for her that whole weekend flooded back. "I don't know what I would have done without you when. . .when Dad died," she said earnestly.

Rance's eyes darkened with emotion. "I'm missing him dreadfully. He was very dear to me, and so is his daughter, Hildie."

"Then if that's the case, do you think you could tell me about Nathan?" Hilda said quickly before she had time to get cold feet again. His face tightened, but before he could utter the sharp retort she saw on his lips, she continued very rapidly, "Something's eating into you, Rance. If Dad had been alive, you'd have been able to talk to him, wouldn't you?"

Rance stared at her. A suddenly wistful look filled his

face.

"I've spent over twenty-three years being taught by Dad," Hilda said very softly. "I think some of his ideas would have rubbed off in that time, don't you?" He remained silent, and she continued earnestly, "Whatever it is, it's affecting your relationship with Jesus, isn't it? You didn't want to say grace that night, and you haven't once offered to pray with me the times you've visited."

"I tried talking to a couple of the church leaders in Toowoomba," he said bitterly. "All that accomplished was condemnation and my ministry there having to finish."

"Did Dad condemn you?"

The anger in his eyes faded. He looked down at his plate and shook his head.

"Do. . .do you believe Jesus condemns you?" she asked bravely.

He raised his head quickly. "No!" he said vehemently. "My de facto relationship with Val was forgiven when I asked Him to be my Saviour. He gave me new life. That old past has been done away with. Since then, when I've slipped up again, I've claimed His promise to forgive me when I agree with Him about my sin."

A sharp pang shot through Hilda. So her name was Val. She swallowed quickly, and quoted huskily, "There is now no condemnation for those in Christ Jesus."

There was an arrested look in his eye. "Your Dad quoted that very passage from the book of Romans, too," he murmured.

A slight smile crossed Hilda's face. "I've heard him remind hurting Christians about that many times. As well as his rebellious daughter!"

"It's amazing, isn't it? I've preached from those words of Paul several times over the years, but its harder to put it into practice when I. . .when I'm feeling so guilty!" he burst out.

"Dad also used to say that after studying the life of the apostle Paul, he had come to the conclusion that he was a man who should have carried the guilt of persecuting and killing Christians to his grave. Instead, Paul wrote those words," Hilda said reminiscently. She looked down at the table, and unconsciously traced a pattern with her fork. "And Paul also wrote to the young man, Timothy, explaining how, despite all his past before he became a believer, Christ still gave him strength and appointed him to His service of ministry."

A strangled sound from Rance brought her eyes swiftly back to his face. He was staring at her with the strangest expression. A vivid blush turned Hilda scarlet. She dropped the fork, and stared at him with dismay. She had been preaching to the preacher!

She opened her lips to apologize, but Rance spoke first. "Thank you, Hildie. I needed to be reminded of that, and I think I can tell you about it all after all. But," he gestured at their rapidly cooling food, "not now, I think. We should get to Normanhurst as soon as possible."

Hilda found she had lost most of her appetite, but forced down the rest of the meal as best she could. She thought that the subject was closed, and as they resumed their journey, she quietly made irregular comments about the traffic and the scenery. Rance hardly spoke, and at last she lapsed into silence.

Unexpectedly, Hilda heard him say, "Hildie, I haven't just been feeling guilty about the immorality in my past. I've been feeling so bad about the type of upbringing my . . .my son has had. What you said about your father's ideas rubbing off onto you stung. I doubt very much if my son has ever been told that God loves him."

"But that's not your fault, Rance!" Hilda cried out indignantly. "You didn't know of his existence."

"No, but I may have if I hadn't cut myself so completely off from Val and all my old friends of that era," he said quietly.

They travelled in silence for awhile. Hilda felt an overwhelming gratitude for the fact that she had always only known a Christian life style. It had saved her from so many painful memories of a background like Rance had known.

"You know, at first I was so zealous about trying to win my friends for Christ," Rance said sadly, "but I was still very young, and even more immature in spiritual things. I found myself being sucked back into their drug scene and lifestyle again. I even. . .one night Val and I again made love. That's what I find so hard to forgive myself for. It was after that night I walked away from them all for good. A couple years later I started studying for the ministry. The years were so busy. I always intended to try and find out what had happened to Val, but then I moved to Queensland."

Hilda was afraid to move as the quiet voice continued. A thrill of delight shot through her. He was telling her at last about himself. He trusted her.

"Just before Christmas, I had a letter from Val's grandparents. They were very worried about Nathan because they had just found out Val had AIDS. As he was my son, wasn't it about time I did something to look after him?"

Hilda gave a choked exclamation.

He glanced briefly at her shocked face and added grimly, "You can imagine that at first I thought it was a hoax. Val came from a family background that. . .well, to put it gently, left much to be desired. Her father was an alcoholic, and her mother had just given up on life and didn't care what happened to her daughter. They kicked her out when she turned fifteen.

"Her grandparents weren't much better, but they did take her in. For years she had refused to tell them who Nathan's father was. They had reared one child, they informed her, and didn't want the responsibility of another. When she had become too sick to look after him, they kept threatening to hand Nathan over to Children Services. So she gave in. They tracked me down at last."

There wasn't a thing Hilda could think of to say as Rance's abrupt explanation finished. At last, when she knew she had control of her voice, she asked softly "Have. . . have you found out why she hadn't contacted you when he was born?"

There was a tense silence, and Hilda wished she had kept quiet as she stared straight ahead, aware that he had tensed even more.

"Yes." That answer was a long time coming. There was so much pain in his voice, Hilda dared not say another word. After a few moments he added in a clipped voice, "She refused to see me until that Thursday before Easter. Then she had the nurse at the hospital ring me. It. . .it was just as I was leaving for the wedding rehearsal. I went down as soon as I could." His voice became husky, and full of self-condemnation. "She. . .she. . .Val told me. . . just before she died, why she didn't burden me, as she put it, by letting me know about Nathan. She thought it would harm me in the church. She. . .she didn't want me to be contaminated by her again because I was a good man, and . . .and it was good to see at least someone she loved escape. . . escape the hopelessness."

Traffic signs swept past, warning that the end of the freeway was imminent. Hilda saw them through a mist of tears, wondering if she could ever have been as noble as that poor woman. And what turmoil Rance must have been in that whole weekend! Hilda couldn't have said a word if her life had depended on it.

"We haven't much farther to go, and I have to concentrate now on finding the Mortons' house. If you haven't been turned off me by what I've just told you, we'll talk more some other time." Rance's voice was withdrawn and unexpectedly cold.

Hilda ached even more for him. So many people he cared about had rejected him because of what he had just told her.

"Nothing you could tell me could ever turn me off you, as you put it, Rance," she blurted out passionately. Anger had cleared her mind and even crept into her voice. Then she suddenly hoped she had not given too much away about her growing feelings for him.

Even as Rance eased his foot on the accelerator in obedience to the speed limit, he reached across and took hold of one of Hilda's tightly clenched hands. Her hand unfolded and then clung to his. Neither said a word as they arrived at the Mortons' home.

Hilda liked David and Kim Morton immediately. They were obviously concerned about Rance, and both gave him big hugs. She found herself included in their loving greetings and felt instantly at home.

It was very late, but at their hosts' insistence they had almost finished a quick cup of tea, when a little voice from the doorway said indignantly "Yous said Unca Wance wouldn't come 'til bweakfas' time!"

Rance's tired face lit up. He put his cup down and moved swiftly to scoop up a curly headed tot and a blue teddy bear almost as big.

"Well, I tricked you, didn't I, princess? Got a kiss for me?"

The gentle love and genuine delight in Rance's face made a lump form in Hilda's throat. He would be a wonderful father. She looked across and caught David's eye. He was watching her watching Rance. A small, surprised grin shaped his lips, and she blushed furiously and bent her head over her cup.

"Jodie, what are you doing out of bed?" Kim said with fond exasperation as she stood up.

The little girl peeped warily at her mother over Rance's shoulder as she hugged him fiercely around his neck. "Jus' lovin' Unca Wance, of course," she said indignantly.

The three watching adults smiled.

Rance chuckled, and his voice was filled with love and emotion as he said, "There, Mummy, a perfectly acceptable answer. But what about I carry you back to bed now so you can get more beauty sleep?"

While he had been talking, Jodie had been staring at Hilda. When Hilda smiled at her, she hid her face shyly and reached up and whispered in Rance's ear.

Rance swung around and stared at Hilda with a startled expression on his face.

A dainty hand pushed on his face trying to turn it back to her. "Well, is she?" the little girl demanded loudly.

"I think you may be one very clever little girl," Rance said very slowly, still staring at Hilda. Then he whispered something in Jodie's ear. He shot a grin of pure mischief at Hilda, and said out loud, "Come on, Miss Moppet, you can meet the pretty lady in the morning. I'd better carry you back to bed before Mummy gets cross with both of us."

"I not Mis' Moffet, silly," they heard her giggle as they both disappeared, "but you're Georthie Porthie!"

The three left behind looked at each other.

"Now, I wonder what that was all about," murmured Kim thoughtfully as she looked speculatively across at her husband. Some silent communication must have passed between them for her eyes widened suddenly, and then she stood up quickly and said, "You must be very tired, Hilda. I'll show you to your room. Rance won't get away from that little madam for awhile, and you can grab the bathroom first."

Hilda followed her obediently, although she too very much wanted to know what had brought that particular look into Rance's face. She was exhausted, but it took her a long time to go to sleep. Not the least of her worries was just when she would see Rance again after he had left her with Jean Drew the next day.

But there was no need to have concerned herself. Rance had worked that out already. "I've rung Jean Drew and told her you're staying here with me," Rance told her crisply after he had said a brief good morning. "David and Kim suggested it."

Hilda stared back at him crossly, even as tingles of relief swept her. "Without asking me?"

"It was the most sensible thing to do. How were you going to find that address on the birth certificate without transport? And I thought you might—" He paused, and looked uncertain for a moment. Then he lifted his chin and glared at her. "I thought that seeing I was so kind as to let you hitch a ride with me all that way, you wouldn't mind helping me with Nathan," he said with a challenge sparkling out of his eyes at her.

Inwardly, Hilda was thrilled. Outwardly, she tilted her

chin right back at him. "And if I do mind?"

He looked taken aback, and she couldn't stop her lips from twitching. Relief flashed into his eyes. He started to smile, but then gave a mock scowl instead. "It'll be bread and water rations for a month!"

"Is this a private joke, or can anyone join?" David's amused voice broke into their shared laughter, and they sobered quickly.

"Just Rance flexing his male chauvinistic muscle," Hilda said cheekily, feeling incredibly light-hearted.

"Didn't get me far," Rance grumbled. He grinned at David and said, "The woman has submitted and will be staying, too. As long as you can put up with us both."

"Good," said Kim as she entered the room with Jodie tucked on one hip. She beamed happily at Hilda. "This is Miss Garrett, Jodie. She's Uncle Rance's friend who came with him last night."

She swung the small girl down. Jodie studied Hilda for a moment and then put her hands on her hips and confronted Rance. "You said she's Aunt Hildie," he was accused.

Hilda watched with amusement as a hint of colour touched Rance's cheekbones. "I'm sure she won't mind if you call her that, princess." He took a long stride forward and tossed Jodie up into the air. "Will you?" he then appealed to Hilda a little uncertainly.

Hilda couldn't resist the two pairs of dark eyes so close together. She swept a deep curtesy. "I'm at her majesty's service."

"Ooooh," Jodie giggled with delight. "I not weally a pwincess! Uncle Wance's jus' bein' funny."

"Funny, am I!" Rance tickled his small captive to her great delight. He then carried her off, at her demand, to play with a new toy.

Hilda turned to David as she heard him sigh faintly. "He's always been wonderful with kids. It's a dreadful shame that—" He stopped abruptly, and bit his lip as he looked at Hilda.

"It's okay," Kim said softly, "Rance told me that Hilda knows about Nathan."

"He's told me some of it, but I think not all," Hilda said slowly, and then she burst out angrily, "How could that woman not tell him he had a son!"

"From what I remember of Rance when he first came to Bible College, she may have been afraid to tell him," David said thoughtfully. "He was a very opinionated, everything's-black-or-white type of person."

"Well, he's certainly not like that now," said Kim fiercely. "He's allowing God to change him into a wonderful man, and a tremendous pastor. Maree's a fool, and the way that . . .that church treated him is a crime! It's really knocked him for a six. His self-esteem is about zero. Seems to think he's suddenly become unlovable and of no more use to God—or man."

"Oh," said Hilda blankly, "I hadn't realized. . ." She stopped short, suddenly remembering what Rance had said about being a failure that night that now seemed so long ago.

"He'll come through this," said David firmly. "I've seen his commitment to Christ stand many tests over the last few years. As long as he maintains his faith and relationship with Christ, he'll find his way soon. We just have to keep supporting him in prayer and any way we can."

Hilda looked at him doubtfully. She knew that all was far from well with Rance's spiritual health. But she said no more, and a little later Rance came back and suggested the worst of the morning peak hour traffic would be over and they should go and see Nathan.

"Does Nathan know you're coming to see him today?" Hilda asked as they neared their destination.

"I wasn't sure how long it would take to wind things up at the church and move my things out of the manse and store them at my step-father's place. And then I couldn't be sure he would get a message from his great-grandparents anyway." Rance looked across at her, and she saw his jaw tighten as he added, "I hope you don't expect a loving father-son reunion, Hildie. He's a very confused little boy, and for some reason, whenever I go near him he retreats."

"What are his grandparents like?"

Rance didn't answer for a moment, and then said grimly, "I'll let you judge for yourself."

The house that Rance parked the car beside was in a very poor-looking neighbourhood. The houses each side were almost sitting on top of each other. Several steps sagged from rotten timber as they approached a front door that had a panel of broken glass, haphazardly boarded up with a scrap of dirty timber.

There was no answer to Rance's first knock. After a few moments, he knocked a little louder. There was a sound of slow, light steps behind the door, and then silence. Suddenly a man's loud, harsh voice roared something out from somewhere in the house.

The door was opened the tiniest crack, and a scared little voice croaked, "Granddad said to go away. He doesn't want any today."

Rance caught the edge of the door and pushed it open a little more. There was the sound of a frightened gasp, and a little figure darted behind the door.

"Nat, it's your father," Rance called softly, "can I see you for a moment?"

There was silence, and then half a face peered around the partly open door. "Oh, please, go away," the boy whispered desperately. "He's sleeping it off, and he'll be so angry if we upset him."

"Then we won't wake him, mate," Rance said in a very controlled voice. "Why don't you just come outside. I want you to meet a very nice lady who's with me."

"No," the boy wailed, "I'm not allowed outside today."

"Rance," began Hilda with dawning horror.

"I know," murmured Rance between gritted teeth. "I saw him too."

He suddenly forced open the door and in one movement grabbed the thin arm of the boy as he started to back off. The boy gave a whimper of pain.

Rance gave a choked sound of distress and changed his grip to gently pull Nathan forward from the dark shadows of the hallway. "Oh, son," he moaned. "Who did this to you?"

One eye was almost closed from a huge bruise that stretched down one side of Nathan's small, tear-streaked face. Blood was smeared on the other cheek, perhaps from the grazes and bruising on both his thin arms.

eight

Nathan cowered, trying to pull away. He was trembling violently. "No, no," his terrified voice begged in pitiful gasps. "Don't hit me. I'll be good."

Hilda moved forward, and crouched down to his eye level. "We would never hurt you, Nat," she said earnestly. "We want to help you."

The pain-filled, childish eyes stared at her. Something flickered across his face and he stopped trying to pull away from Rance.

"Wouldn't you like to come with your father? He'll never let anyone hurt you ever again," she persisted very gently.

The boy looked at Rance, and then quickly back to Hilda. "For real?"

She nodded earnestly, trying desperately to keep the tears from her eyes.

"And. . .and will you be there, too?"

"Yes," Hilda said firmly.

He studied her suspiciously for another long moment. Hilda could feel the tension in the tall, grim figure beside her and prayed that he would not let his fury show. Nathan glanced fearfully up at his father briefly, and then back at Hilda. He nodded once, and then he staggered, all the colour that was left in his face suddenly leaving it.

"I feel sick," he muttered.

Hilda's hand went out to steady him, but Rance was before her. His strong arms reached down to carefully pick up the boy. Nathan stiffened with terror again, and then suddenly went limp.

Without a word, Rance took off with him down the steps. "Get in the car, Hildie. He's fainted. You can hold him. I'll drive." The words were staccato sharp.

Rance settled his burden as gently as he could on her lap. As he started to move rapidly to the driver's side, there was a sudden roar of expletives from the house.

"Hey, what'd ya think—" The words were cut off as the bedraggled, bleary-eyed, and bloated man in the doorway saw Rance turn toward him.

"Yes, it's me, you filthy old man," Rance shouted furiously at him. "And don't think I won't be back!"

Rance turned away, but Hilda saw the sudden fear that twisted the old man's face. He opened his lips and mouthed something back which Hilda could not make out above the sudden roar of the motor. She thought he had said, "It's not my fault." Hilda looked down at the still body in her arms.

As the car pulled away from the curb, Rance said sharply, "Can you get the street directory out of the glove box?"

Nathan was undernourished, but still a dead weight against her shoulder. "No, I can't Rance," she said urgently, "I don't want to move him."

"Right." Rance pulled up around the corner out of sight of the house and quickly found the directory. "I know there's a public hospital in this suburb somewhere," he muttered fiercely. "Ah, there it is. This should only take about ten minutes."

It was a little more than that before they pulled up outside the emergency entrance. As the car stopped with a jerk, Nathan stirred and tried to sit up.

"It's okay, Nat. It's okay," Hilda soothed him. "We're at a hospital. There'll be a doctor here to make you feel better."

Fear flashed into the dark eyes that looked up at her again, and Hilda understood why when the casualty nurse took one look at the boy in the arms of the tall, ashen-faced man, and greeted him by name.

"Well, if it isn't Nathan again. Been in a fight again young man?" she said suspiciously as she looked from him to the man carrying him.

"You might say that," the grim-faced Rance said so savagely the woman took a step back. "But it certainly wasn't with someone his own size!"

Her expression softened. "We thought that might have been the case before," she muttered softly.

"Before!" Rance snarled. He visibly controlled himself and deposited Nathan very gently on the examination couch. Then he said in a tight, sharp voice, "I need to use the phone immediately."

The nurse nodded, "I'll show you and tell the doctor. Be right back," she added to Hilda.

She waited for Rance to precede her, but he hesitated. A large hand reached out and touched the unbruised cheek so tenderly, Hilda felt the tears spill over the top at last. For Rance's sake, she was pleased that Nathan didn't shrink away from that loving touch. He just stared blankly up at his father.

"Don't be scared, mate. You are never going back to that house again, Nathan. Never!" Rance said fiercely, and then strode away.

By the time he had returned, a doctor had started to gently examine Nathan. "You the boy's father?" he scowled at Rance.

Rance nodded briefly, and as the doctor finished his examination, stood rigidly beside Hilda. Her hand crept out and touched his tense hand. He jumped slightly and then grasped her hand tightly, never taking his eyes from the small body. They both winced as bruise after bruise was revealed all over the thin little body.

All the time, the doctor asked Nathan soft questions. Some the boy answered, some he didn't. At last, Rance cleared his throat and took a step closer. The doctor paused. He frowned and looked up at Rance intently.

"Nathan, we want you to tell this doctor exactly how you got hurt. Then it will be easier to make you better and make sure it never happens again."

"But. . .but you said I'd never have to go back. You promised," the weak voice managed. "It won't happen if he never comes near me again."

"If who never comes near you, young man?" the doctor asked conversationally.

"Why, Granddad of course!"

No one moved for a moment. Then Hilda saw the doctor relax and look compassionately for the first time at Rance. Suddenly, Hilda realized angrily that he had thought Rance must have done it!

Rance crouched down and looked the boy straight in the eye. "Nathan, no one is allowed to hurt another person like you have been, especially a boy your age. Don't you know that?"

The boy just stared at him blankly.

Rance continued, "The police won't let them, and I've just rung them up. When you're feeling better, they'll want to ask you all about it, and you must tell them the whole truth. Do you remember what I said last time about coming to live with me?"

There was a faint nod. "He. . .he said you didn't mean it."

"Oh, son, I've already missed out on too many of your

years. There's no way I'm going to miss out on any more!" Rance vowed in a cracked voice.

Then he bent over and placed a soft kiss on his son's forehead. Hilda felt the tears sliding down her cheeks again, and then caught her breath as a thin hand suddenly reached up and touched Rance on the cheek. When Rance stood up, he was smiling down at the boy gently.

"Okay, you two," the doctor interrupted briskly. "This young man needs a couple of X-rays, and then I think we'd better find him a bed here for awhile." Instant fright flashed into Nathan's eyes. "You're still suffering from shock as well as feeling very sore," he added firmly, and then said quickly, "Oh, your Dad and this young lady can stay with you if you want them to."

Nathan looked anxiously from Rance to Hilda wordlessly.

"Of course, we're staying," Hilda said determinedly. "As long as you want us to."

The relief that filled his face before he wearily closed his eyes brought a choked sound from Rance.

"That's settled than," the doctor said cheerfully, "but now there's not much room in this little cubicle, so they have to wait just outside while the nurse cleans you up a bit. She's going to give you an injection too, so it doesn't hurt so much when we move you."

Once out of earshot, Rance burst out to the doctor, "The nurse said he's been in before?"

The doctor nodded grimly. "Not quite two weeks ago, an elderly woman brought him in. Claimed he'd been in a fight, but he was so scared that we were suspicious."

"Why didn't you report it to the police then?" Hilda asked angrily.

"We reported it to Children's Services for them to investigate. I had hoped they would have been out to the home by this." He sighed. "Like all of us, I suppose" he added wearily, "not enough staff and too many urgent calls."

Nathan was kept sedated for the next few hours but still slept restlessly. The moment his eyes opened, they searched anxiously for Rance and Hilda. Reassured by their smiles and touch, he would doze off again.

Once when he was asleep, the police called in briefly. It was obvious they had already talked to the medical staff. After introducing themselves, the officers explained that a warrant was being issued for the arrest of the great-grand-father.

Tight lipped, Rance snarled, "Good!"

Hilda observed the darkness in his face with considerable worry. She had been silently praying during their vigil, as much for this anguished man as for his son.

Sometime later, Rance murmured to Hilda, "Do you mind staying without me? There are a few urgent things I need to do. Tell him I'll be back as soon as I can."

A little surprised, she stared up at him and then nodded. She felt the warmth of his lips brush her own and then he disappeared.

Rance was gone for longer than she had expected. When Nathan woke a few minutes after he left and realized his father was gone, Hilda would never forget the look of despair that filled his face.

"Look, he's got to come back and take me home, doesn't he?" she hastened to reassure him.

He stared at her for a moment with a flicker of hope, but then his face closed up again. His resigned look of disbelief nearly broke her heart. How many people all his life had abandoned him to cause that total look of unsurprised acceptance?

The colour had returned to Rance's face when he did

return. She turned swiftly to greet him and was relieved at the gleam in his eye.

"Oh, I'm so thankful you're back," she burst out.

It had been a long, exhausting few hours. Nathan had been awake for some time, but she had not been able to get a word out of him. She had tried to quietly talk about anything she could think of, but he had just turned his back on her.

"Hello, Nathan," Rance said with a piercing look at the face that had briefly turned to see who had entered.

Hilda thought she saw surprise, followed by relief, flicker across the battered face, but then he turned quickly away again.

"Sorry I was away so long, but I've been very busy— very successfully busy, I might add," Rance said with a quick smile at Hilda. He winked at her and raised his voice slightly. "Hildie, God's been looking out for us. What would you say if I told you I've just organized a fully furnished house to live in with Nathan?"

"Already!"

The previous evening, Rance had told the Mortons that after seeing Nathan, he intended searching for a flat or unit to rent so the boy could go and live with him as soon as possible. The Mortons had warned him that such a search could take some time. Anything worth living in was very expensive at the moment, and there were long waiting lists for any rented premises.

Rance smiled a little grimly at Hilda, and said quietly to her, "David was right. There's absolutely nothing decent enough to rent anywhere. So, for the first time in my life, I've rung up my step-father and taken him up on his repeated offers of help. When he got over his astonishment, he made a few phone calls. It turns out he owns a holiday house that has just become vacant."

The tense little body in the bed suddenly turned over painfully, and stared at Rance suspiciously.

"Do you like the beach, Nathan?" Rance asked gently.

A faint glimmer of excitement touched the battered face. "I. . .I don't remember."

Hilda gave a little gasp. She saw Rance's hands clench tightly. Very few children in this land of sun and surf, living so close to the sea, could say that!

"Well, the house you and I are going to is right near the beach. As soon as the doctor says you're well enough, we'll go there," Rance said in a controlled voice. "It's a long way from here. It's down the south coast on the way to Wollongong."

"Will. . .will he know where we are?"

Rance moved closer and placed a hand on the boy's hand. "Nathan, the police have told me that your. . .your grandfather's been arrested. He couldn't get any bail money, and he's locked away in a jail cell. You don't have to worry about him ever again."

His voice was gentle, but Hilda heard the steel in it. She shivered. This was a Rance she had not seen before.

"Will you be there, too?" The dark eyes beseeched Hilda.

Hilda looked at the boy, and then up at Rance helplessly.

A hard light glinted at her from suddenly fierce eyes that dared her to contradict him. "Yes," he said firmly, "Hildie will be there, too." When her eyes widened and flashed back at him, he added autocratically, "Don't worry, there's a live-in housekeeper, according to my step-father. You won't have to do anything."

"Exactly where is this house?" Hilda said stiffly.

"Near Stanwell Park."

The name meant nothing to Hilda. Darkened amber eyes

clashed with clear blue eyes.

"It's on the south coast, but north of Wollongong. Its well-known for the hang gliding off the cliffs not far from there. The house is actually at a place called Wattle Point, but there's also a beach, even if it's only a small one compared to your Goldcoast standards." He paused and then pleaded softly, "It's obvious that Nathan's wary of me. Perhaps it's because he's only known unpleasant men. And who knows what he's been told about parsons! I need you, Hildie."

Hilda looked swiftly away, hoping her face had not revealed the suddenly desperate feeling that filled her. How she longed for him to need her for so many other reasons than to help with Nathan. She looked across at the tense little figure in the bed.

"Looks like we three stick together, then, doesn't it, Nat?" she said with a forced smile.

Nathan's face brightened with hope, but he didn't smile. He studied her face carefully and then doubtfully looked briefly at Rance. He closed his eyes and muttered listlessly, "I suppose."

Hilda glanced up at Rance, and saw him biting on his bottom lip. He would have a battle on his hands for Nathan to be convinced that he really cared what happened to his son.

The doctor called back late in the afternoon to tell them there were a couple of cracked ribs, but fortunately no other damage except the lacerations and bruising. When they told him about the house at Wattle Point, he agreed with some relief that Nathan could be discharged the next day as long as he was still doing all right.

Hilda felt emotionally drained by the evening. She felt relieved when Rance decided that rather than stay all night at the hospital, they would get a good night's sleep at the Morton's so that they both would be better able to cope with moving Nathan the next day.

"He's going to have to learn to trust that when we have to leave him we'll always come back," Rance said grimly.

It was a relief to go back to the Mortons' and be fussed over by Kim. They insisted on going down to Wattle Point the next morning to make sure everything was set up for them.

"You don't need any hitch at this stage," David said firmly. He grinned suddenly. "Besides, what a great excuse for a day at the beach, even if it is a bit cool!"

The next morning, Hilda was very quiet and thoughtful on the way to the hospital.

Rance glanced at her a couple times, and then said shortly, "Wishing you hadn't agreed to help me?"

Hilda looked at him steadily. "No, not for a moment, Rance. But I was wondering when I'd have a chance to start looking for my. . .my mother."

"I've already said I'd help you," Rance said impatiently, "but Nathan comes first."

Hilda was silent. This Rance was different from the man she had thought she was getting to know. There was an increasing hardness, a coldness about him that worried her immensely. As they approached the ward, this concern intensified. Rance muttered something angrily under his breath when he saw the old, shabby woman at the nurses' station.

He lengthened his stride as her loud, angry voice reached them. "I demand to see him. He's my only great-grandson. How dare you—"

"They dare because, as next of kin, I insisted they don't let anyone near him. Especially you!" barked Rance.

"You!" spat the small, withered woman as she turned awkwardly around to face the new obstacle. "And where were you all these years, hey? When my poor little girl needed a father for her son, where were you, hey? You religious people are all the same. All talk, talk—"

"That's enough!" Rance said furiously. "Your daughter keeps his existence from me, and you allow my son to be bashed up by that miserable excuse for a man you call a husband, and you dare, you dare—"

"Don't you talk to my gran like that, you big bully!" cried out an angry, trembling voice. "He bashed her more'n he did me!"

The love that transformed the old woman's pale face tore at Hilda's heart. "Oh, my lamb," she cried out in a shaking voice, and dodged past Rance to stumble toward Nathan as he limped down the corridor. "Oh, what did he do to you? What did he do to you?"

Nathan's face crumpled, and then it was hidden as he was wrapped so very gently in the small woman's arms.

Rance took an angry step forward.

"Rance, wait!" Hilda grabbed at his arm. "We're the strangers here. She's all he's had for a long time," she whispered urgently. There had been something else worrying her, too. "And there was something about her that—"

"Gran, are you all right again, now," they heard Nathan's tearful voice say.

"I will be, love, I will be."

But even as the now faint voice tried to reassure him, they saw her stagger. Hilda darted forward. As small as his grandmother was, she was still too heavy for Nathan to hold. As Hilda reached her, the older woman crumpled into a heap on the floor.

"See what you've done now!" screamed a frantic Nathan

at Rance. "She's been in hospital!"

The slight figure Hilda was crouched over opened her eyes and tried to sit up. Hilda was frightened by the grey skin and bluish lips. She looked up frantically at the nursing sister as she joined them.

"That's no way to talk to ya' Dad," the old lady gasped painfully. "You be a good boy for him, now, ya' hear?"

"Don't try and talk," the nurse said sharply.

A hospital trolley arrived swiftly. A white, grim-faced Rance helped the wardsman lift the frail body.

As he went to move back, a withered hand reached out. "So sorry," the whisper of a voice said. "He. . .he took it out on me 'cause I took Nat to hospital the other week. . . after. . . after he hit him."

The nurse tried to hush her again, but her grip on Rance tightened. "He's. . .not bad man. Never touched him before. Just. . .the drink. Upset 'bout Val. So glad ya' came back."

The nurse had her fingers on the woman's pulse and nodded urgently to the wardsman. The trolley started moving, and Hilda grabbed for Nathan as he started after it.

"Not now, Nathan," she said tearfully. "Let them look after her first."

The rigid figure stared up at her, tears streaking his cheeks. "But she'll want to see me," he protested, and then turned belligerently to Rance. "And you can't stop me. When you didn't turn up or write, Granddad got upset, and he started drinking. She got punched because of you, and he hurt her bad. I don't want you for a father. Oh, why did you have to come! I hate you, I hate you!"

nine

As the car pulled into the driveway at Wattle Point and Hilda saw David Morton coming quickly towards them, she gave a silent sigh of immense relief. She never wanted to live through such a tense few hours again.

Opening her door almost before the car cruised to a stop, she stepped out and greeted him loudly. "Hello, David, we're here at last!" As she reached him and held out her hand, she muttered through gritted teeth, "Please do something before I strangle them both!"

David gave her a keen look and moved over to open the back door. Hilda heard him draw in a quick breath as he saw Nathan's poor battered face glaring at him.

"Hello, Nathan. I was beginning to wonder where you all were," David said calmly. "I thought my old friend must have become lost trying to find his way through the city traffic."

Nathan didn't stir. His arms were folded and he merely glared silently back. Rance slammed his door with unnecessary force and marched around to the trunk.

"This is Mr. David Morton who we've told you about, Nathan," Hilda said quietly.

"If my daughter can call your father Uncle, it's only fair for you to call me Uncle David," David said cheerfully. Ignoring the lack of response, he added, "Why don't you take your time going up to the house, while I help with your gear?"

Nathan still didn't stir. David gave a slight, imperceptible shrug at Hilda and moved away.

She knew how bitterly hurt Rance had been by his son's outburst at the hospital. He had been withdrawn and cold ever since. First of all, Nathan had refused point blank to leave the hospital while his gran was so sick. When she had regained consciousness enough to weakly insist he go with his father, she had produced the key to the house for them to go and pack up Nathan's pitifully few personal belongings.

Their arrival at the house with a reluctant, still belligerent boy had precipitated another fight. Rance had taken one look at the few clean-but-worn clothes and coldly dictated there was no need to take any clothes—only school things, toys, and books.

One small boy had one large amount of pride. "What's wrong with my stuff?" he'd shouted back.

Hilda could see how upset Rance was by the state of the house generally, as well as by the ragged, stained clothes. But she could also see the fear Nathan was trying to hide at the thought of not having old familiar things with him in his new life. At last, Hilda had persuaded Rance that Nathan would not be well enough for a few days to take on a massive shopping spree, and should take a basic wardrobe. She pretended not to see the few forbidden items that Nathan threw in the boxes when his father wasn't looking.

Now, as Hilda stared at the angry, rebellious boy, suddenly she'd had enough, both of him and his unreasonable father. "Oh, you poor little darling, can't you manage to undo your seatbelt?" she said in sugary tones. "Here, let me help."

"I'm not a baby," snarled Nathan.

"Then stop acting like one," she snarled right back, "or I'll treat you like one."

His eyes widened slightly, but he didn't move, just eyed her warily. She started to reach for the seat belt button. He pushed her hand away, and in a moment was standing beside her. She returned his glare with good measure. His eyes faltered and he looked away. Then she watched an awed expression transform his sullen features. He had suddenly spotted through the trees the panorama of white sands and blue, tumbling surf.

The peace of the scene was a tremendous contrast to the battle royal that had been taking place between Rance and his son. Hilda joined him and felt her own annoyance and frustration start to drain away.

"God's handiwork is rather wonderful, isn't it?" she murmured as she too drank her fill of the beauty.

Hilda was aware that Nathan turned toward her, but whatever he was going to say was interrupted by a gleeful little shout.

"Unca Wance, Unca Wance, where's you been? We been waiting and waiting to build a sand house."

Jodie came racing along the steep path from the house. She ran toward Nathan and demanded, "Are you Nafin?"

As he stared at her, she suddenly stopped still. Her eyes widened, and her mouth drooped. "Youse poor, poor face." She went right up to him, and reached up on tip-toe and tenderly kissed his cheek. "Is better now!" she proclaimed and then whirled toward her father as he hastily approached. "Nafin's hurted his face, Daddy," she said tearfully.

David picked her up and glanced apprehensively at the rock-like figure of the small boy who was staring at the dainty little girl with dazed eyes. One hand had gone up to the spot on his cheek where she had kissed him.

"Yes, he has, princess, and that's why he needs a nice rest here at the beach," Rance's voice said unsteadily.

He had moved next to David and was watching Nathan. Nathan took his eyes off the little girl and looked at his father.

Rance smiled at him gently. "And I think he'll need lots of kisses to help him get better."

Nathan's eyes filled with tears. "I. . .I—"

"It's going to be all right, son." Rance dropped the case he had been carrying and took a few long strides. He crouched down in front of the boy and kissed him on the cheek in the same spot Jodie had. Looking him in the eye he said "I'm sorry. I wasn't angry with you—just angry at myself. I should have accepted my mother's offer to help me clear up things in Queensland, and come down sooner, or taken you back with me. And I did try and ring, but the phone was disconnected."

Father and son searched each other's eyes. Then Nathan's face crumpled. As she saw Nathan suddenly fling his arms around Rance, tears started trickling down Hilda's own face. Her love for this complex man who could apologize to a small boy like that grew by leaps and bounds. Then she stood transfixed as the words started tumbling out of Nathan.

"I waited and waited," the boy sobbed. "I had all my stuff packed up. You didn't come. Then he started drinking again. He. . .he called Mum all kinds of horrible names. I told him to shut up, and he swung at me. Then. . .then he hit Gran real bad. I couldn't wake her up, and. . .and the lady next door rang the ambulance. . .and when he woke up and she wasn't there he went sort of wild, and started hitting and kicking at me. I hid all night. . .and. . .and. . . ." The jerky, disjointed words broke off and he suddenly wailed, "Is Gran going to die, too?"

David gestured to Hilda as Rance started to quietly speak

again to Nathan. She took the trembling little girl from her father and started back to the house. David grabbed a couple cases and quickly followed them.

"Why was Unca Wance and Nafin cwying?" Jodie said with a big sob of her own, looking back over Hilda's shoulder.

"Because they have both been cross with each other," Hilda managed, as she hurried the little girl away. "They . . .they're both going to need lots and lots of our loving to help them."

Several days later, Hilda remembered those words a little grimly as she watched Rance and Nathan trying to have a game of cricket on the firm, wet sand. She was acting as a reluctant wicket keeper, while Rance bowled gently to Nathan.

She gritted her teeth as a too cheerful, too easy going Rance called out, "Watch out for this spin ball, mate!"

Nat put up his brand new bat and patted it gently away. "Boy, Dad, that had a great spin on it," he said with a beaming smile.

If only they would stop being so polite to each other! If only Rance would start going easy on trying to give his son everything at once! Rance bowling far too easy balls, and Nat's false appreciation of his expertise was so typical of the last few days.

I never dreamt that one day I'd want to see a father and his son have a good family disagreement, Hilda thought angrily.

But she knew that this state of affairs could not last. They were both too tense from trying too hard to be the perfect father and son. Rance had bought fishing gear and taken Nathan fishing. Nathan had been excited and hugged his father. Rance had bought him this cricket set. Nathan had been excited and hugged his father. She knew from something Nathan had said one day, that he hated cricket, preferring soccer.

The housekeeper, Mrs. Burkett, had turned out to be a pleasant, middle-aged woman who lived in an attached small flat with her husband. She cheerfully bustled around, insisting to Hilda that she didn't need any help at all except after tea each evening, when she left them to clear away. So Hilda had traipsed along after father and son on all their excursions. They had both insisted on her going with them, and she knew they felt more secure with a third person present, so had gone along with it all.

It's time I had a good talk with this perfect father, Hilda thought grimly, listening to Rance's anxious apology for bowling too fast, as Nathan missed a ball.

"Okay, that's it. I've had enough cricket," she called out as she lobbed the ball back. "I'm going back to grab the shower first."

She ignored their protests and started running up the beach. As she reached the path that wound its way up a steep slope through light bush to the house, she glanced back and wasn't surprised to see Rance pulling out the cricket stumps as they prepared to follow her.

Hilda had become more and more annoyed with Rance, too. He knew how anxious she was to drive into Sydney to the address on her birth certificate. She had taken the street directory out of the car and looked up the address in front of him. He had just briefly commented that he had thought it would be in the inner city area. Just over an hour's drive away, he had informed her with a frown.

The main part of the beach house was not large, a basic three bedroom brick veneer, but with excellent kitchen and bathroom facilities. Rance had seemed a little surprised that it was not larger, and had confided that it was much smaller than the other two houses his step-father owned, one on the Goldcoast, and the other on the Sunshine Coast, north of Brisbane.

Sunday had come and gone with no mention of finding a church to attend. Hilda had shrugged to herself, knowing that Rance was falling over backwards to let Nathan not be upset or put out about his father being a minister. Instead, they had travelled down to Wollongong and gone to the movies. Hilda knew it didn't hurt to miss one Sunday at worship, but it still disturbed her as another indication of Rance's spiritual life not being what it should be. They did not even say grace before their meals.

Hilda had retired early that Sunday night, and read a long passage in the first letter by the apostle John in the Scriptures. It was all about love, and it drove her to spend a long time in prayer.

Now, as far as Hilda was concerned, her holiday had come to an end. Nathan's bruises were still fading in places, but most had already gone. The cuts were healing well, and the swelling on his face had subsided quickly, leaving only a yellowing bruise over his cheek bone and a yellow tinge in one eye. What she knew would take much longer to heal was the bruising on his soul and spirit. And that healing process could take even longer if Rance did not soon come to his senses.

Hilda made straight for the phone.

"Yes, of course you can stay here tonight, Hilda," Jean Drew's crisp voice said. "I've been looking forward to seeing you very much. I'm off duty tomorrow, and was even considering taking a run in the car down there to see you all."

Hilda had showered and was in her room packing when

she heard Rance's brisk footsteps and then a knock on her door. She took a deep breath and closed her eyes for a moment before calling out, "Come in, if you're game!"

"That sounds ominous," Rance's amused voice said as he opened the door.

Hilda didn't turn around and continued placing a pair of jeans in the half-filled case on the bed. Rance had come to an abrupt standstill. There was silence, and at last she swung round to face him. He looked from the case to her face and back again.

"You're packing," he said flatly.

"Yes," she said crisply and turned her back on his accusing glare. "I rang up, and there's a train from Helensburg in just over half an hour. If you can't drive me, I'll ask Mr. Burkett next door."

There was another long pause before he said very quietly, "Are you going to stay with Jean?"

Hilda turned around slowly. There was a sick feeling in the pit of her stomach. She wondered for a moment if he had any idea how difficult it was for her to leave. "I've just rung her. I don't think you and Nathan really need me here any longer, and I do have business of my own to attend to."

"Not need you!" Rance burst out. There was a hint of panic in his voice. For a moment, Hilda's heart took a flying leap only to plunge back to earth with a thud when he added urgently, "Nathan can hardly let you out of his sight. For some reason he still can't relax with me unless you're there."

Hilda hesitated for a moment, and then choosing her words carefully she said earnestly, "He's not the only one who can't relax. You're both trying to be someone you're not. Rance, I've tried to tell you, you're trying too hard!

You both need a bit of time to yourselves. Let him go and play on the beach by himself if he wants to. You go and read a book if you want to. You don't have to spend every waking moment in each other's hair."

"But we've wasted so much time, Hildie." Pain darkened his eyes. "There are so many years to make up."

"But you can't make them up," Hilda said earnestly. "Can't you see, you've got to learn to accept each other as you are at this point in time. Let the past go, Rance."

Rance raised his eyebrows. "Is that what you're doing, Hildie?"

Hilda looked away and then sank down on the side of the bed. Why did her mother give her away? Who was she? So many unanswered questions!

"What past!" she said at last with a touch of bitterness. "I don't know enough about what happened to be able to say. Perhaps I never will, " she added sadly and looked up at him pleadingly. "But I have to try, Rance. I can't let go of what I know so little about."

"But that's what you're asking me to do." He walked away from her, and stood looking out of her window. With his back still turned, he said in a tortured voice, "Nathan is old for his age in so many areas. He's lived with his mother all his life until last year. Her lifestyle was something I ran from so I wouldn't be corrupted, and yet my son has lived it for nine years! What's he seen? What has he done? What's been done to him? Val told me she didn't know for sure where or how she was infected with the HIV virus. She was only actually diagnosed three years ago. Apparently she never told a soul until last year the truth about her bouts of illness. It could have been needle sharing or. . .or . . ." His voice choked, and he hunched his shoulders.

Hilda stood up and went over to him. For a moment she

hesitated, and then she said shakily, "Rance, you only did what the Bible says about running from temptation. That's called obedience. If you had stayed, perhaps Nathan wouldn't have a father to love him today."

There was a long silence, then Rance turned toward her. He reached out slowly and caught her by the shoulders. Searching her eyes intently he whispered, "And I would never have met such a beautiful woman. That's twice now you've been God's messenger to me." He took a deep breath and added simply, "Thank you, Hildie."

Hildie wasn't sure who moved, but she felt his arms slip around her as his lips descended to lightly taste her lips. All her love spilled out as she opened to him, and then they were crushed together, and suddenly passion was a white heat that leapt between them. As it had before.

The moment was timeless. It felt so right, so natural to feel his lips move over her face, back to her lips gently as the flames died away. Then they just held each other, savouring their closeness until Hilda moved her head from his shoulder and looked into his face.

"Don't you dare apologize for that kiss," she said with mock sternness.

Rance was very serious. He ran a finger under one of her wayward curls and pushed it back, not taking his eyes from hers. "Hildie, you're so very sweet, but I'm still not sure if either of us is ready for this."

Hilda stiffened, and her arms dropped. He immediately released her, and she backed away a few steps. Ready? She loved him. It was that simple.

"Is. . .is it Maree?" She asked in a stifled voice.

Surprise flashed into his face. He took a step towards her and then stilled at the sound of running steps outside.

"Hey, Dad, Hilda! Mrs. Burkett says tea will be on the

table in half an hour. Dad! Where—"

Without thinking, Hilda called out, "We're in here, Nat," and swung away from Rance to fling the bedroom door open.

Nathan stared at her with startled eyes, and then looked at Rance as he appeared behind her. The expression on his face changed as he looked from one to the other. Disillusionment was followed by bitter disappointment. "I thought you two'd be different," he said scornfully.

Hilda didn't understand for a moment, and then her eyes widened in shock. Before she could say anything in their defense, he took off.

"Nathan, wait!" Rance pushed her out of the way and raced after him.

Hilda started to follow, and then stopped. Returning to her room, she made for the mirror, and gasped. Her lipstick was smeared. Her lips were slightly swollen. She was still flushed, and in fact her whole appearance was such that a worldly wise nine-year-old boy could tell she had been well and truly kissed! Besides, that lipstick must have transferred to Rance.

She grabbed a tissue and wiped her lips. A quick comb restored her tousled hair, and then she went to find father and son. They had not gone far.

As Hilda paused at the entrance to the back patio, she heard Rance say firmly, "I don't care what you know happens in bedrooms, Hildie and I were doing nothing wrong. I like her very much. She's my friend, nothing more."

A knife slashed at Hilda's heart.

Nat swung around from staring down the back yard and said with a sneer, "Yeah, yeah, friends have pasho kisses all the time!" He saw Hilda in the doorway, and turned away again.

Rance hesitated. He glanced over at Hilda. Perhaps he saw something in her face that betrayed her pain at his word "like." She didn't want him to merely like her as a friend, she wanted him to love her enough to. . .to. . .

A large, but gentle hand reached out and turned Nathan around. "Nathan, you know I'm a minister, don't you?"

Nathan's lip curled. *I wonder who he's copying,* thought Hilda sadly. It was such an adult expression.

"I think you've been given some very strange ideas about ministers, and merely getting up and preaching, and all his talking about God doesn't mean that minister's never make mistakes, Nathan." Rance smiled ruefully. "I know that only too well since I found out about you."

Suddenly he looked over at Hilda again. "Come here, Hildie," he said quietly, "I want you here so Nat can know you agree with what I want to say." When she had joined them, he crouched down to Nathan's level and looked him in the eye. "Hildie and I probably weren't very wise being in her bedroom together, but we would not do anything there, or anywhere else for that matter, that is wrong in God's eyes."

As Rance continued in a very firm, convincing voice, Hilda saw doubt flicker in Nathan's face. "It's not that Hildie and I are different from anybody else. We may want to make love together as married people do, but we would never do that because we both love our Saviour, Jesus Christ, too much, and we know it would hurt Him."

Amazement washed over Nathan's face. "You really believe all that stuff?"

Hilda's heart leaped. Rance merely asked, "What stuff do you refer to, Nat?"

"'Bout God loving the world and Jesus dying on the cross, and. . .and all that."

Hilda held her breath. She heard the slight tremble in Rance's voice as he calmly replied, "I certainly do believe that God loves everyone in the world, and that includes me and Hilda, and you, too. Jesus came and showed us what God's like, and told how God wants us to live. Then He died and rose again, so we could have our sins forgiven and have God as our loving Father to be with us for always."

"Where did you hear about Jesus?" Hilda asked gently.

Nathan looked up at her and scowled. "Mum told me, and then she made me go to a dumb Sunday School last . . .last year. Gran said it was all nonsense, and I didn't have to, but Mum got real angry and upset with her." Suddenly he grinned. "The picnics and Christmas party was beaut though."

"Doesn't anybody want their tea tonight?" a rather cross voice said behind them.

Hilda swung around. "Sorry, Mrs Burkett! I'm starving. I don't know about these two." She glanced at her watch, and looked ruefully at Rance. It was too late to try and catch the train to Sydney.

Rance caught her eye, and smiled understandingly. Her heart reached out to him, and his smile broadened. There was a glow about his face she realized she had not seen for many, many months.

He stood up. "We won't be a moment, Mrs Burkett, and thank you very much. You go on home, we'll be okay." As Mrs Burkett disappeared, he looked down at Nathan uncertainly. Then he looked back at Hilda pleadingly.

"Hildie has to attend to some very important private business in Sydney, and she's put it off to stay with us and help us get to know each other better. I went to tell her that the Mortons are coming for the day tomorrow. Would you mind very much if I drove Hildie to Sydney while you stayed and kept Jodie out of mischief?"

Alarm flashed into Nathan's face. "You'll both be back to sleep tomorrow night?"

Rance looked silently at Hilda. She glanced from one anxious face to the other, and her heart melted. "My goodness, you two do look alike!"

Both faces lit up. Their smiles were very similar. The tall fair man and the small boy turned to look at each other. "We do?" There was sheer wonder and delight in Rance's voice.

Hilda laughed gently at them. "Now Nat's face is almost back to normal, you sure do. But it's not just your faces. It's more in your expressions." She shook her head at them, thrilled to see how pleased they both looked. "And the answer is yes. I'll have to ring Jean again, but we'll both sleep back here tomorrow night."

The instant relief that flooded Rance's eyes warmed her through and through. Then a shadow touched her. Would she know more about her mother this time tomorrow night?

She pushed the thought away. "Keeping up with you two trying to be the great Aussie cricket captain and his main spin bowler has made me very hungry," she said firmly. "So let's eat!"

ten

The Mortons were disappointed when they arrived mid-morning to discover Rance and Hilda were only waiting for them before they left for Sydney.

"But we still hasn't made our sand house, Unca Wance," wailed Jodie.

"I'll help you build a sand castle," Nathan offered gruffly.

Big eyes studied him doubtfully for a moment, and then Jodie beamed. "Now?"

"Whoa, young lady," Kim laughed. "Hat, sun block, and a tee-shirt first. Even if it isn't summer, you'll still get too much sun, knowing how long it takes to build one of your masterpieces."

Rance was still smiling as they drove up the winding road toward the Prince's Highway. "That Jodie!" he chuckled. "She's devastating at three. By the time she's twenty-three she's going to cause havoc in the male population."

Hilda laughed with him, but felt a little wistful. She hoped Jodie never lost her innate sweetness. Looking back over her teenage years and brief stint at university before her mother's illness had brought her home again, she knew she had often been too self-opinionated and abrupt to be very popular with either sex. Perhaps that was one of the penalties of being a spoilt only child. She had always vowed to have more than one child if she ever married.

Hilda glanced wistfully at the man beside her. Then she deliberately turned from those particular hopes and dreams and back to their destination and all it could lead to.

Hilda didn't realize how long she had been silent until Rance asked in a gentle voice, "Worth a penny?"

She looked blankly at him, and then smiled a little sadly. "I haven't heard anyone say that since Mum died." She took a deep breath. "I was just wondering if my. . .if she's had any other children by now."

Rance was silent for awhile, then he said in a troubled voice, "Hildie, sweetheart, have you faced up to the possibility that your natural mother may not want to meet you, let alone allow you to meet any of her family?"

Hilda swallowed. How could she tell him about the sleepless nights, and the times of agonized praying? "I. . .I've told God that I'll leave it in His hands to sort all that out, Rance," she said at last in a low voice.

"Oh, Hildie, I've never known a woman like you!" Rance burst out. Startled, she looked across at him, but before she could take in what he had said, he added in a quieter voice, "We haven't talked about last night. I meant what I said to Nathan. It was a mistake kissing you like that in your bedroom."

A mistake! The memory of that kiss had sent her to sleep with hope and love and a smile on her lips. And he called it a mistake!

"If you say sorry one more time for kissing me, I'll. . . I'll. . ." she said through gritted teeth, and then snapped loudly as he started to protest, "I don't want to talk about it. I've got other things on my mind today."

They had reached the intersection with the Southern Freeway. Rance was silent as he speeded up and eased into the traffic. Feeling bitterly hurt at his calling a mistake what she had believed was an earth-shattering experience for both of them, Hilda stared out at the passing traffic through a blur of tears.

As Rance eventually started to speak, she kept her head averted. "I'll go along with you for today, Hilda. But we are going to talk about how we feel about each other very soon." Rance's voice held an unexpected hint of steel. "Just one more thing for you to think about. When David rang me last night, he said that a church in Brisbane had been trying to contact me. Apparently they want to know if I would be interested in entering into discussions with them about a possible ministry there."

Hilda turned to him at that, but as she opened her mouth to say how pleased she was for him, he added quickly, "But we aren't going to talk about that either today. Today is something I've kept you from doing far too long. I am sorry about that, Hildie. It was very selfish of me."

"No, no," she protested with tears in her voice. "I could have said something before this. I. . .I. . .Oh, Rance, I'm been so scared that for awhile I was only too glad to put it off."

Rance's hands clenched, but he did not reach out to comfort her. Instead, he said strongly, "Didn't you just tell me you've put it all in God's hands?"

Hilda's sudden fright subsided. "He loves me and won't let anything happen to me that He and I can't handle together," she murmured at last. "I remember a certain minister saying that in a certain sermon earlier this year."

She threw a smile at him, and he grinned. A slight tinge of red touched his cheeks, and she heard the pleasure in his voice as he said, "Well, wonder of wonders! Someone was actually listening to the preacher!"

"No, no," she laughed, relieved they were getting back on their old footing. "You've got it wrong again, Preacher! I was listening to the Holy Spirit speaking to me through the lips of the preacher."

"Ouch! Putting me in my place!" Rance chuckled and then he sobered and added with awe, "You know that's pretty incredible, isn't it? He uses us so many times to bring a word of comfort to people when we often don't know how they're hurting."

Hilda hesitated, and then said steadily "And He even uses the Vals of this world sometimes when they don't claim Him as Lord. Although I wonder about Nathan's mother. Perhaps something you said years ago did bring her to some faith. She must have been a pretty special person, Rance."

"She was. Especially when we first met, but then. . ." Regret filled his voice. "She never once mentioned sending Nat to Sunday school. Not that we had much time to talk. She was too ill, and every breath was an effort. Last night he told me she insisted he had to go because his father would have wanted him to know all about that 'stuff' as he calls it. It thrills me to think perhaps all my zealous foolishness so many years ago bore some kind of fruit. I always thought my slipping back into my old lifestyle would have invalidated everything I tried to tell my friends about God." Rance snorted with disgust at himself. "Apparently Nathan's been wondering why I haven't mentioned anything about God to him before this."

"So that's why we said grace at breakfast time!"

Rance looked at her a trifle sheepishly. "I've been pretty stupid, haven't I?"

"Well," she drawled, "I'm not so sure about the pretty bit, but I'll give you the stupid part."

He gave a loud laugh. "I'll go along with that. And that's exactly why I need you around!" She stiffened, and he added swiftly, "But, as I said, all that can wait until later."

Hilda forced herself to relax again, but the rest of the

way, the thought remained. What did he mean by "all that" in connection with needing her?

When they reached the inner suburb of Paddington, they had to stop a couple times to consult the street directory. At last, after taking a couple wrong turns, they pulled up slowly outside the right address. They got out of the car and stared at the four story building silently, and then looked at each other.

"A hostel," Rance said doubtfully. "Are you sure this was the right street?"

"Well, that sign way down the hill said it was," Hilda replied slowly. She straightened her shoulders. "Only one way to find out."

It was the right address. And no, it had always been a hostel or boarding house, and no, the owner did not have a clue where they could find the people he'd bought it from a couple years earlier.

"And they hadn't owned it that long anyway. I believe the people before them used to put up all types. Sorry can't help youse folks," the unshaven, unwashed superintendent smirked. "The place was a real dump when we bought it a few years ago."

As they reluctantly returned to the car, Hilda muttered, "I hate to have seen it when it was what he calls a dump."

"Me, too," said Rance grimly. "I'd sure call it one now. The smell was dreadful." He looked up and down the narrow street with its rows of old terrace houses, and sighed. "So we start on the neighbours as that lady at the adoption place suggested."

A long, long time later, they closed the gate of the last house in the block and silently started back to the car. Rance sympathetically slipped his arm around the weary, bitterly disappointed Hilda and hugged her. "There's still the electoral roll books, sweetheart."

"With a name like Jones? And we don't even know if it was her real name!" she replied despondently. "I've had enough today. Let's go back and spend some time with the Mortons before they have to go home."

The days were getting shorter, and when they arrived at Wattle Point the sun was very low. It had already slipped behind the hills west of the small village on the coast. There was a strange car parked besides the Mortons' red Camry, but although the house was unlocked there was no one there.

"That's strange, surely they'd be back getting ready for tea by this," frowned Rance. "Not even Mrs. Burkett's here. I wonder—"

"Look," said Hilda urgently. She pointed to a figure racing up the path from the beach. "That's Aunt Jean. Let's meet her, I think something must be wrong."

"Oh, thank God you're back," gasped a pale Jean, as they reached her. "Nathan and Jodie have been missing for over three hours."

Rance's face drained of all colour, but he just stared at her silently. Hilda slipped her hand under his arm and clutched him tightly.

After she had regained her breath sufficiently, Jean explained. Nathan and Jodie had raced back to the beach straight after a snack to finish their sand castle. Kim and David had sat in the outdoor furniture where they could watch them.

"When I drove up, they had both dozed off. They said it must have only been, at the most, half an hour," Jean told them rapidly, "At first we weren't too concerned at the two not being in sight. Apparently they'd been scavenging, out of sight at times, for things on the beach to decorate the castle. It wasn't until we strolled down to the beach that we realized they were no where to be seen."

"Did you say three hours ago?" rasped Rance.

"I. . .I arrived about three hours ago," said Jean reluctantly. "A lot of people have been helping us the last hour or more, including the. . .the life-savers."

Three hours! Hilda looked out at the vastness of the ocean. She couldn't bear the anguish on Rance's face.

"Have. . .have you rung the police?" she asked unsteadily.

Jean was watching Rance. "That's why I was coming back when I saw you arrive."

"Why did you wait so long!" Rance cried out. "They could have been swept out to sea anywhere by now!"

"No!" Jean said sharply. "At first we thought they may have gone for a swim, even if it's been too cold since you arrived here for anyone without wet suits. That's why we alerted the surf club, and it turned out someone from their observation deck had been watching the kids. They saw them running toward the track back through the sand hills. We've been searching the sand hills and the next beach around the headland.

"A while back, a couple of fisherman returned and told us that, when they were parking their car, two kids like them raced past. It was the car park at the other end of the beach. We even thought they might have gone to the little shop near the main road for an ice block or drink, but no one's seen them."

"As far as I know, Nathan never had any money," Rance said with difficulty. "Has anyone been searching the bush the other side of the road?" he asked urgently.

Jean shook her head. "Not to my knowledge."

Hilda drew in a sharp breath. There were only a few houses there, set way back in the bush. The terrain sloped fairly sharply up toward the mountain range. Thick under-growth underneath towering trees hid many dangers for adults. And they were only children. It would be so easy for them to lose their way.

"But they both loved the beach. Why would they want to go somewhere else?" said Hilda with a puzzled frown.

"Who would know with kids," Rance said briefly and started for the car. "I'll go take a look anyway."

Without a word, Hilda raced to climb in beside him. He glanced at her gratefully, but didn't speak.

Hilda's mind filled with stories she had heard of children lost in the harsh Australian bush. But that was usually in the ranges or the outback. *Surely not here,* she thought with a shudder. *Not so near this little beach resort.*

One single-lane driveway ended at a large brick house set close to a steep cliff. It looked deserted and was guarded by a snarling German shepherd.

"The children would certainly have turned away from here," declared Rance as he turned the car.

"I certainly hope so," Hilda said with a shudder at the thought of the dog terrifying Nathan and Jodie.

The next driveway was much shorter and ended at a small, rundown dwelling of unpainted weatherboard.

"Been here all day," said the elderly man who came out to meet them. "Would have seen them if they came this way."

He followed Rance back to the car and peered in at Hilda. "Sorry, missus," he added gently, "hope your kids'll be okay. It's pretty thick bush around here. I sure wish I could help you look." He thumped his chest. "Old ticker, you know. But I'll sure offer up a prayer or two for your son."

As they drove off, the tears Hilda had been holding at bay spilled over. She realized how much she had grown to love that small boy who so often reminded her of his father. A deep desire to be able to truly call him her son started to burn within her. She wiped the tears away as unobtrusively as she could, but Rance still saw them.

"They'll be all right," he said grimly as they waited for traffic to pass before pulling out onto the main road again. "God hasn't kept Nathan all this time to let something happen to him now." Suddenly he pointed. "That looks like a walking track through the bush. What about we park the car and try along there?"

They walked as quickly as they could along the rough track. Every now and then Rance roared out Nathan's name, and they stopped to listen intently. At times, overhanging foliage almost blocked the path, pulling at their clothes, scratching their arms. It was getting darker. The sun was long gone behind the mountains.

"Do you think they really could have pushed this far through here?" Hilda asked doubtfully.

The track had suddenly became much steeper and rougher as it wound still higher up the mountain.

"I suppose not," Rance said despondently. He yelled out once more, "Nathan! Jodie!"

Hilda froze. Rance looked at her. Then they both heard it again.

"Dad, Dad? Is. . .is that you?" A faint voice sounded in the distance, and then louder, urgent! "Jodie! you get back here! Jodie! The bunyip'll get ya'!"

Rance and Hilda were already running as fast as they dared on the rough ground. Then a tiny figure raced around a bend. The little face was streaked with dirt and tears as it hurtled into Rance's arms.

Jodie was too breathless with sobs and fright to speak for a moment. Hilda tore past them.

Then, as Rance hurried after Hilda with his burden, Jodie sobbed breathlessly, "Nafin's hurted. He won't walk, Unca Wance."

When Hilda reached Nathan, he was trying to crawl over a large rock. His clothes were ripped and torn, and as she knelt down, he groaned and fell back. Rance reached them, and put Jodie down. As Nathan stared speechlessly up at his father, his face was white and filled with fear. He actually cringed away from Rance, and a horrified Hilda realized that he expected Rance to hit him.

Hilda was tremendously proud of Rance as he passed Jodie to her and wordlessly scooped up the small boy in his arms. He held him tightly, rocking him ever so gently. After a moment he said in a trembling voice, "Oh, son, son! Don't you ever scare me like this again!"

Hilda was cuddling the quivering Jodie tightly. "What's happened to your legs, Nat?" she asked gently.

"Nafin felled over," Jodie sobbed.

"Shush, darling. He'll be all right now his daddy's here," Hilda murmured and searched for a handkerchief to wipe the little face.

Rance had put Nathan down and was quickly examining him. "I twisted my ankle on a stone and busted my other knee when I fell," Nathan gasped painfully.

Jodie had stopped crying at last and wriggled out of Hilda's arms. She stuck both hands on her hips and glared down at Nathan. "See! I'se told you and told you I had to find our daddies!" She turned to Rance and gave another quivering sniff. "He hunged on to my jeans and wouldn't let me go! And. . .and then he told me 'bout the bunyip," she accused, and then peered uneasily around into the bush.

Hilda's lips twitched. "The bunyip? I thought they were monsters that only lived near billabongs," she said straight faced. "I don't see any water around here!"

"Of course they are," Nathan said crossly. "And they're only in fairy stories anyway!"

"Ooooh, you told a lie!" accused Jodie angrily.

"You'd have got lost or done somethin' stupid like bein' hit by a car crossin' the road like you nearly did before," yelled Nathan furiously. Tears rolled down his cheeks. "Oh, Dad, she wouldn't do what I said!"

"But we'se did see a koangawoo, Nafin! Jus' like I said!"

Hilda began to see light. "You came into the bush to see a kangaroo?"

Rance glanced at Nathan sharply. He looked away guilt-ily from his father's eyes and down at the large handker-chief Rance had just tied over the bleeding and swollen knee.

Jodie nodded vigourously. "Nafin's never ever seen a koangawoo. But he has now!" she added triumphantly.

"There was a small one just near here, Dad," Nathan burst out with an excited gleam in his eye. He pointed to a small grassy area in through the trees. "He was eating the grass. We were real quiet, but he started to hop away, and . . .and I—"

"He twied to catch him, and he felled over," Jodie chipped in.

"I wasn't trying to catch him—" Nathan started to say angrily, but Rance cut him off firmly.

"Let's talk all about what happened when we get you back to the house. Your Mummy and Daddy are very, very worried about you, Jodie."

Rance hit the horn as they neared the house, and in a few moments Jodie was in her mother's arms. There were more tears from Jodie when Kim started to cry as she clutched her daughter to her. But David was furious.

He rounded on Nathan. "How dare you take a tiny thing like Jodie across that dangerous road and into the bush like that! What on—"

"David, that's enough!" Rance said sharply as he paused from lifting Nathan from the back seat. "I think it may have been the other way round!" He swung around and continued to the house with his precious burden cradled gently in his strong arms. Jean hurried after him.

Hilda paused briefly and said gently to the angry David, "Let's look after them first, and then we'll sort it all out."

The two children were popped straight into hot baths. Mrs. Burkett fussed around, feeding them all after Nathan's ankle and knee had been attended to. Jean declared his injuries appeared to be sprains. Jodie fell asleep and was put down on a bed before they let Nathan tell them what had happened.

Jodie had been horrified when she had found out he had never seen a kangaroo, even at the zoo. Hilda was appalled too, at this further revelation of the restricted life he had led.

Then Jodie had insisted they had to find a kangaroo. He had willingly followed her until he realized she wanted to cross the main road and go into the bush on the other side. When he had refused, she had suddenly taken off, narrowly being missed by a speeding car coming quickly around the nearby bend.

"Boy, she was like greased lightning," Nathan said earnestly, "I yelled and yelled at her, but she just waved at me to follow and ran toward that track."

By the time he had been able to cross safely, she was a fair way into the bush. When he had caught up to her, he admitted that he thought they might as well go a bit farther. Then he had been so excited at actually seeing the small kangaroo, which the adults privately thought might have been a rock wallaby, he had tripped over the rock and gone sprawling. He had managed to crawl a little distance, but that boulder had defeated him.

"I had to hang onto her tight, and threaten her with all kinds of things to stop her tearing off again," he said with a sniffle, fighting back the tears. "She could have got lost or hit by a car, or. . .or anythin'."

Hilda felt a tug of pity for the small boy as he finished, and looked anxiously at David and then his father.

"I'm very sorry Jodie was so naughty, Nathan," David said quietly. "She knows she's not allowed to cross a road by herself. We're just thankful God answered our prayers and kept you both safe from worse harm."

"You're. . .you're not mad at me anymore?" Nathan asked tearfully.

"Far from it!" David said remorsefully. "I'm just so sorry I yelled at you. Afraid it was as much sheer relief you were both okay. Rather, we can't thank you enough for looking after her as you did." He turned to Rance, and now even Nathan could not have mistaken his moist-eyed sincerity, and Rance's pride, as he said, "Congratulations, Rance! That's some boy of yours!"

Nathan stared at the two men in astonishment, and then his pale face blushed crimson. After the Mortons had carefully carried the still sleeping Jodie off home in their car, he asked hesitantly, "Uncle David's a minister like you, isn't he, Dad?"

Rance nodded, looking at him closely and then glancing a little apprehensively across at Hilda and Jean. It was the first time the boy had mentioned his profession.

"Are all parsons like you two?" Nathan asked with a puzzled look on his face. "Sayin' that about prayin' and bein' sorry and all that."

Rance relaxed. "Not only parsons do those things," he said gently and then grinned. "But it's a different matter if you mean are parsons like us because we're charming, full of fun and," he sobered, "love their crazy kids, and get worried sick when they do a disappearing act."

Nathan's face crumpled. "I'm sorry, Dad," he whispered, and then added louder with awe, "You. . .you were really worried about me?"

Rance swallowed, and his voice was choked as he said, "What do you think? I do love you very much." He added in a stronger voice, "And if you ever dare go off without telling me again, I'll be forced to ban all television for. . . for life, probably!"

Nathan's eyes widened and then he grinned back for a moment before suddenly yawning mightily.

"Right! Bed for you." Rance stood up and went over to pick him up.

Hilda hesitated, longing to have the right to go with them as Kim had when David had carried Jodie to bed.

"Night, Hildie," Nathan said sleepily over Rance's shoulder. Then they were gone.

"Well, I suppose I should be going soon," Jean said and started packing up some dirty plates. "Perhaps we should get these out of the way first. I'm sorry I came on an impulse to see you in one way, but glad I was here to help look for those two darling little mischief makers." She paused and looked a little anxiously at Hilda. "The Mortons said they didn't have a clue why you both tore off to Sydney today. Is everything all right, Hilda?"

Before she knew it, Hilda was pouring the whole story of her adoption and search out to the astounded Jean.

"I knew you'd been born at my old training hospital,"

Jean exclaimed when Hilda had fallen silent, "but your parents never gave a hint you were adopted. And you actually know your natural mother's name?"

Hilda sighed wearily. "Well we aren't even sure if it's her real name or not, not with Jones as a surname. It was Margaret Louise Jones on the certificate."

Jean dropped a pile of cutlery on the floor with a clatter. Hilda looked up to see a very strange look on her face. "Did. . .did you say Margaret Louise?" Jean asked sharply.

"Yes, I did," Hilda said slowly. Jean suddenly hid her face as she picked up the cutlery again. "What's the matter, Jean?"

Jean finished collecting the cutlery, and started for the kitchen. She tossed over her shoulder, "Oh, I'm just tired and clumsy tonight. Thought I'd heard that name before, that's all. But, as you said, I guess its a pretty common name."

Rance arrived in the dining room just then, and Jean grabbed her bag soon after and left rather abruptly.

Hilda thoughtfully watched the red glow of her car tail lights disappear. Suddenly she felt chilled. As Jean had touched Hilda's arm when she kissed her good-bye, her hand had been noticeably trembling. Suddenly, she didn't believe Jean's casual explanation about dropping the cutlery. Something about the name Margaret Louise Jones had upset her.

Hilda rubbed her arms against the cold wind sweeping off the sea and turned to go back inside. A set of headlights slowed, and turned into their short driveway.

She turned back with a grin. The efficient Sister Jean Drew must have forgotten something. Her heart quickened. Unless Jean had changed her mind about talking about what had upset her.

But the car wasn't Jean's, and a tall, willowy blonde climbed out and stood up. Hilda's heart plunged. The woman strolled with a confident swagger over to where she was standing, in a stunned silence, at the foot of the steps.

"Hilda Garrett?" softly drawled Maree Sadler, Rance's ex-fiancée, "Rance's mother told me I'd probably find you here with him and that brat of his. Too bad, sweetie. You lose. He's mine."

Then she swept regally up the steps past the still motion-less Hilda, to fly toward the man who had appeared in the open doorway of the house. "Rance, darling! Oh, darling, I just couldn't stay away. I'm so pleased for you."

Then her arms went up around Rance's head and she very enthusiastically kissed him.

eleven

Hilda's heart sank still further the next morning when she arrived at the breakfast table and Rance greeted her with a radiant face.

The night before, she had not been absolutely certain whether Rance had been pleased or not to see Maree. He had certainly let Maree plaster her lips on his, Hilda had thought with a scowl. He had certainly been extremely polite and friendly, until Hilda had pleaded tiredness and left them alone to share the supper she had prepared. Maree's triumphant smirk had kept her awake for hours, long after she heard her car drive off.

She forced an answering smile to his happy one. "How's Nathan this morning?"

"A bit stiff and sorry for himself, but I don't think we need to take him for X-rays," Rance beamed at her. "Hildie, the most marvelous thing has happened."

Hilda thought her heart would break in a million pieces if she actually heard him put into words that he was going to marry Maree after all. She cleared her throat and said swiftly, "Yes. . .yes, I know. I'm very happy for you, Rance."

He looked a little puzzled for a moment, and then he beamed again, "Oh, Maree told you, I suppose. Isn't God good!"

If He was giving Rance what he wanted so much to make him look like this, than yes, God was being very "good" to him, Hilda supposed.

But what about my love for Rance, Lord! her lacerated heart cried out.

Aloud she said rapidly, "I've decided I'll be going home today, Rance." Dismay filled his face, and she hurried on before he could protest, "I doubt very much if I've much hope of finding my natural parents, and I shouldn't make Jim and Gail wait any longer to tie up things with our solicitors. I'm booked on a flight from Mascot. Can you take me to the airport, or should I get a train to Central and the Mascot bus?"

"You've given up your search," he said slowly. "And that's why you look so unhappy."

"For the present, yes," Hilda said quickly and forced another smile, completely unable to tell him he was wrong. It was the thought of not seeing him and his son everyday for breakfast for the rest of her life that was devastating her.

Nathan scowled savagely when she told him she was leaving, and only brightened up when Rance assured him firmly they would see her again before much longer. He looked warningly at Hilda when she turned sharply toward him. She glared back, but obeyed his unspoken demand not to protest.

"And what about we go and see your gran after we drop Hildie off at the airport?" Rance asked him. He had been very quiet since reluctantly agreeing to take Hilda to the airport. "She's been home from hospital a couple of days now, and you can pick up any of your other belongings you want that we left behind before," he added a little gruffly, to Hilda's delight.

Although Nathan was able to limp painfully without assistance, he agreed to wait in the car while Rance went into the airport terminal with Hilda. "We will see you soon, won't we?" he asked with a trembling lip as she kissed him good-bye.

"Sometime," was all she could manage huskily. She gave him a fierce hug and whispered, "I'll always love you though."

Rance waited with her in the queue while she bought her ticket and had her bag weighed. Hilda risked glancing at him a couple of times. He was grim and remote.

As they at last moved away from the counter, she said quickly, "Don't come up to the departure lounge, Rance. You mustn't leave Nat waiting too long. I'm so pleased you're taking him to see his grandmother."

"Hildie, I. . .I. . ." Rance swept a hand through his hair. "Why are you rushing away like this?" he asked with a hint of desperation in his voice. "You know it's probably going to be weeks, if not months before I can leave here. I didn't tell Nathan, but the police rang this morning and want to talk to him. I haven't a clue how long before the court case comes up and—"

"And you'll manage very well without me here," she said with false cheerfulness. "Nathan already loves you very much. You're probably in for a few more tussles with each other, but you'll work it out." She stopped awkwardly, not at all sure how to say good-bye.

Rance knew. She suddenly found herself wrapped tightly in his arms. His lips desperately devoured hers, and for one blissful moment she kissed him back hungrily. Surely Maree wouldn't begrudge her this last kiss.

Rance showed no signs of releasing her, and at last she wrenched away. Blinded with tears, she spun on her heel and walked swiftly away, forcing herself to ignore his choking protest. The taste and essence of him on her lips had to be savoured for the very last time.

Her self-control was very precarious, but she dared a quick glance back from the top of the escalators. He was still standing rigidly where she had left him, a dreadful scowl on his face. When he saw her watching him, he hesitated, then gave a quick salute. As she stepped off the moving stairs and he disappeared from sight, she heard a shout. She thought she heard him say, "Bye, darling," but knew she must have been mistaken and kept walking blindly toward the security check.

♨

Rance was right about the court case taking many weeks to come up. The long, lonely weeks crept by. At first they were only enlivened by a few phone calls from both Rance and Nathan. Rance's letters were friendly, never containing a word about that traumatic good-bye. Hilda rarely answered them. She had decided that last kiss had been one of gratitude, even affection, but she still felt ashamed and guilty for responding so whole-heartedly. After a while, he rarely contacted her, leaving her with very mixed feelings.

When she had first arrived home, she had insisted that Jim let her do some work on the property. He had studied her pale, drawn face and reluctantly agreed. So she drove the tractor occasionally and worked hard in her garden. Then she offered her help with the young people's work at the church and found herself enjoying her involvement at church more than she ever had before.

Hilda missed her father and Polly tremendously, yet as she spent more and more time in reading the Scriptures and applying the promises with faith, the pain continued to lessen. But no matter how busy she managed to be, there was a deep core of human loneliness that only one person could assuage.

She still wondered about her natural parents at times and knew that one day she would have to start the search again. For the moment, she just needed to be in her old, familiar surroundings to sooth her heartache and to try and find out what God wanted her to do in the future. This included wondering about returning to university. The closing date for applying for a place the next year loomed closer, and she knew a decision would soon have to be made.

It was a good season so far, although they could have done with more good falls of rain. The wheat that Jim and his workers had planted grew tall. When the freezing westerly winds swept across the flat paddocks, the waves of green often reminded Hilda of the waves of the ocean as seen from the beaches at Wattle Point and Stanwell Park.

And through it all, Hilda's longing and love for Rance never diminished. Her ever-growing relationship with Christ was the only thing that sustained her through some grim days. Day by day she had to rely on Him to keep going, especially after a letter or a phone call from Rance.

Then one day another letter from Rance arrived. Or rather, Hilda realized, it was a brief note enclosed with a letter from Nathan. Rance wrote "I've agreed to accept the offer of the church in Brisbane. My longing to stay in the ministry has only increased these past weeks. I start early in the new year."

Hilda was thrilled for him, knowing how much he wanted to serve Christ in that way, and she was relieved that by the comments Nathan made, he, too, was looking forward to the move. They had continued to live at Wattle Point, but Nathan had not enjoyed the small school he had been attending after being used to the large city school. Hilda took a deep breath as she carefully placed the letters with the other small pile in her drawer. Knowing she would have to wait even longer to see them again made the following days seemed lonelier and the nights longer.

Unexpectedly, regular letters from Jean Drew had arrived over the weeks since Hilda had returned. They were always chatty and loving, and Hilda began to find that it was easier and easier to tell Aunt Jean, as she still called her, more and more about her good and bad days. Rance was rarely mentioned, and Maree never.

She was a little surprised that there had not been a whisper about Rance and Maree's engagement being renewed. Then she realized they must be waiting until he could leave Sydney. At the Government Children Services insistence, Nathan had been going regularly to a counsellor. Nathan's grandfather had pleaded not guilty due to diminished responsibility for his actions. Twice the court case had been postponed, much to Rance's disgust.

Winter gave way to an early spring. Then the large old peach trees, that Bob Garrett's mother had planted so long ago, began to spread their carpet of blossoms over the black soil and the green lawns. The heat of the sun increased, and a few scattered storms refreshed crops across the plains.

One particular day, Hilda returned late in the afternoon from a trip with the Stevenses to the annual Carnival of Flowers in Toowoomba, always held in late September. She had not been to watch the huge Carnival's procession for many years and thoroughly enjoyed it. It was a very hot day, and on the way home, Gail and Jim teased her about her sunburned nose and cheeks because she had forgotten to take a hat.

As they pulled up, Jim cocked his head and said, "I think your phone's ringing, Hilda."

Hilda groaned, but as she started to rush from the car, the phone stopped. She shrugged and turned back. "If it's important enough, they'll ring again."

Gail smiled at her sympathetically through the car window. "Have a cool shower and you'll feel better."

"Tanks are getting a bit low," Hilda smiled back. "Thanks a lot you two. It was great fun."

"I'm glad, Hilda," Gail said seriously. "You haven't had a very happy time these last few months."

Hilda forced a smile, but could find nothing to say. The car rolled into motion and soon they were gone. A tremendous feeling of bleakness filled Hilda as she entered the house. Was she always going to feel as empty and lonely for Rance's company as she did now? Today would have been so wonderful to share with him.

O, Lord, I thought I might be starting to get over him by now, she prayed silently as she took Gail's advice and had a shower. *What am I going to do?*

As she dressed, she knew the answer. Keep trusting God, as she had been. Keep letting Him strengthen her day by day, as she had been. Keep serving and loving Him. Keep submitting to His will for her life.

"But some days, it's so much harder than others, Lord," she suddenly pleaded out loud, as she looked in the mirror and wearily brushed out her wet hair. "I get so lonely for even the sound of his voice on the phone."

Then she froze. There was a loud knock on the front door. She still hardly ever thought to lock it, even though friends had warned her she should now that she lived alone. The sound of the shower must have drowned out the noise of a vehicle. She put down the brush on her dressing table and was half way to the door when she heard him.

"Hildie, where are you?"

Her feet suddenly had wings. "Oh, Rance, Rance!"

His face lit up with pleasure as she flew toward him. It

was the most natural thing in the world to feel his arms close around her, and feel his lips burning a trail of fire all over her face before settling on her lips.

"Well, really, you two! It's about time!" another familiar voice said with a wealth of satisfaction in her tones.

Hilda lifted a dazed face, and stared. "Aunt Jean, you . . .you. . .," she managed almost incoherently, from the heaven of Rance's arms. "And Nathan? Is he here, too?"

Jean's face suddenly lost its smile. "No, he's still over with Marian for the moment. We. . .we thought it best. . . that is. . ."

Hilda suddenly realized she was still hanging on to Rance for dear life, and tried to push away. "Oh! I shouldn't have. . ."

"And don't you dare say you're sorry," laughed Rance. His eyes were blazing triumphantly. He gave her another hug, and dropped a quick kiss on her nose before allowing her to slip out of his arms. Then his expression also sobered as she went to greet Jean.

A little breathless still, a thoroughly bewildered Hilda looked from one to the other. "What is it? What's happened? Why didn't you bring Nathan? Is the court case over?"

"Whoa," Rance smiled, but this time, she noticed the smile didn't light up his face. "One thing at a time. First, yes, it's all over, in that the old man was given a suspended sentence because of his deteriorating health and age."

"Because you insisted your barrister bring a plea for clemency," Jean said abruptly.

Rance looked a little embarrassed, and shrugged. "Well, I ended up feeling pretty sorry for him. He's old, and even these weeks in custody were punishment. After all, he had lost a granddaughter he loved in his own fashion."

Hilda took a deep breath, and plonked down on the nearest chair as her legs gave away. "And Nathan?"

"Oh, he's just great. He's changed a lot." Pride and love filled the father's face. Rance moved nearer to Hilda, and suddenly he was so grave, she froze. He sat down beside her and picked up her hands. Then he said very quietly, very earnestly, "Hildie, darling, Jean's got some news for you. It's about your natural mother."

He had called her darling.

Her eyes pleaded with him silently, and then began to glimmer with tears as she read the unmistakable message in his eyes. She was his darling, and he loved her.

"Later, darling," she thought she heard him whisper.

He stood up and beckoned to Jean. Hilda saw her look pleadingly at Rance. He shook his head very slightly, and then Jean suddenly moved and sat where Rance had just been sitting beside Hilda.

Hilda tensed. Margaret Louise Jones? What could Jean . . .?

Jean was very pale. Her hands were clenched tightly in her lap, and she was staring at Hilda with the strangest expression.

"Aunt Jean! You. . ." Hilda looked back at the still figure of Rance, and her eyes grew puzzled, and then widened with excitement. "You've found out about my mother?"

He shook his head slightly, and his voice was choked as he said, "I haven't. Jean has." His sudden look at Jean was very gentle and full of compassion. "You should tell her, but I will if you can't."

Jean was very still, looking down at her hands. "No," she said shakily at last, as Hilda began to wonder if she was going to speak at all, "I have to tell her."

Then an incredible thought struck Hilda. "Are you. . . are you. . .?" she whispered.

Jean looked up quickly. She stared at Hilda, and then she said wistfully, "No, I'm not your mother, but I so easily could have been." She took a deep breath. "Margaret Louise Jones was my only sister."

Hilda stared at her. She swallowed, and opened her mouth, but nothing came out.

"And we're so very sorry, Hildie, sweetheart," Rance said softly as Jean also seemed stuck for words, "but she died very soon after you were born."

There was silence, and then Hilda's eyes filled with tears. "She. . .she died?"

Jean nodded, tears rolling down her cheeks.

"And my father?"

"Roger Jones was a wonderful man." Jean swallowed painfully. "He's the only man I ever loved, but he loved Margaret," she said simply. "I thought Margaret never knew, but now I'm not so sure. It might be why she never told me she was pregnant. When they set their wedding date, I couldn't bear to see them married, so I managed to get a position at a hospital in London to do my midwifery training. Only a few days before the wedding, Roger was killed in a boating accident. I. . .I didn't know that for a long time."

Hilda gave a little moan. How dreadful to lose someone you loved like that. She looked up at Rance, and he crouched down beside her, taking her hands tightly in his.

"I. . .I was very bitter and angry when I was in England, even blaming God for my misery," Jean continued, staring sadly into the distance. "I was very lonely over there at first. My resentment and frustration alienated me from making friends. I cut all ties with old friends here, even

Marian. Margaret had written me a couple of letters soon after I left. I couldn't answer them, and when they stopped about the time of the wedding, I wasn't worried. I was so utterly self-centred that I felt only relief not to be reminded of all I had missed out on."

She looked so wretched, that the watching Hilda slipped a hand from Rance and reached out to place hers over the clenched fists of the older woman.

Jean turned sadly to her. "By the time my twelve months training had finished, I had made a few good friends and decided to stay there longer. I wrote to Margaret then, but the letter was never answered. It was almost three years before I returned, and it seemed as though Roger and Margaret had disappeared from the face of the earth. Mutual friends told me about Roger's accident, but Margaret had moved to Sydney soon afterwards and they had lost track of her. I. . .I hadn't heard her name since you told me your mother's name the other night."

A sob shook Jean's body. "I found out a few days ago that you were born eight months after Roger was killed. All this time I thought I had no one, and I can't get over the fact that I never even knew there had been a baby, my niece."

Hilda thought of the broken-hearted young woman finding out she was pregnant. That cheap boarding house in Paddington must have been her only alternative.

"So she must have wanted me after all," Hilda said huskily.

"Oh, yes, she wanted you all right!" Jean said fervently. "You told me you were born at my old training hospital. I always maintained my hospital was the best there was. Margaret must have deliberately moved to be close to it so you could have the best of care. A couple of the nurses who looked after her told me she'd said something about her sister training there."

"You've spoken to nurses who. . . who. . .?"

Jean nodded briefly. "I've kept in touch with a few old friends from those days. Between us, we were able to work out who would have been working in the obstetric unit when you were born." She swallowed, forcing back the tears. "I. . . I had to be certain it was my sister. It's taken me a long time to track anyone down. But staff did remember you because it was all so tragic; one woman losing her baby and never able to have another, and one mother so thrilled to have a baby to remind her of the man she loved, and then dying herself before she could tell them your father's name. Apparently the Garretts fostered you for a long time before they were finally allowed to adopt you when no relatives could be traced."

"Poor Mum and Dad," Hilda whispered. "Perhaps that's why Mum became so paranoid about telling anyone I wasn't their own daughter. She was terrified I'd be taken from them."

Jean nodded again. "More than likely. You see, Margaret told the hospital staff her name was Jones, but it wasn't her legal name, and they had nothing else to go on. She had only been at the boarding house address a couple of weeks and no one knew where she had come from. There weren't any relatives to make inquiries. Even Roger's folk didn't bother to find out how his fiancée was after a couple of months. Probably too painful a reminder."

Jean gave a huge sob. "I don't know if I'll ever be able to forgive myself for letting my envy and resentment cause me to be so heartless and unforgiving toward my sister. Even since I became a Christian a few years ago, I've deliberately kept this part of my life buried deep down. I don't know how God can forgive me!"

"Oh, Aunt Jean—" Hilda stopped, and through her own tears, she suddenly started to smile. "Aunt Jean," she murmured very slowly, and then she said it louder, "Aunt Jean! Oh, all this time you've been my real aunt after all!"

She began to laugh and cry, and suddenly she and Jean were holding each other tightly.

"Oh, don't you see?" Hilda cried, "It's so wonderfully incredible! Of course God's forgiven you! Only He could possibly have arranged for you to have known me since I was a little girl. He gave me parents who loved Him and could teach me about Him. I've even called you Aunt all this time!"

twelve

When Jean and Hilda surfaced from their tears and joy, they realized Rance had disappeared.

"The poor dear," Jean smiled shakily, "he's had a real cot case on his hands for the whole trip. I knew you'd be so disappointed that. . .that your mother and father had died, and. . .and I didn't know how you'd feel about us, and—"

"Oh, Aunt Jean!" Hilda gave her another hug. "I've thought you were absolutely marvelous, for almost as long as I can remember." She gave her a shaky smile. "These last couple years especially." The wonder in her voice was reflected in her shining eyes. "To think it was you who stayed with me when I so desperately needed someone after Dad died!"

"God's ways are perfect," murmured Jean with awe.

"They sure are!" Rance's voice exclaimed behind them.

He was carrying a tray with three steaming mugs. As she thankfully sipped her drink a few moments later, Hilda thrilled that he'd remembered just how she liked her tea. Suddenly a wave of shyness mixed with delight swept over her as she filled her eyes with him. Then her euphoria faded. There was still Maree. She glanced down at the cup in her hands.

"And you, Rance," she murmured with difficulty. "What's been happening with you?"

"You mean, besides trying to keep Jean here in order?" He grinned at Jean.

Hilda was startled. "You mean, you knew?"

"I didn't know what to do," Jean smiled gently back at Rance. "This lovely man was there, and I knew how much he thought of you, so I ended up pouring my suspicions out to him. He's driven me all over the place these last couple months."

"Months!"

Rance's beautiful smile reached deep into Hilda's susceptible heart, and her love for him flared brighter still.

"Yes, it took a long time. A couple of Jean's friends were on an overseas trip. Then we flew to Perth to talk to someone else."

Hilda was beyond words. He had been prepared to go to that time and expense for her.

"The nurse who was with Margaret when you were born has been living there for many years. She's a grandmother herself, now," Jean said quietly. She put down her cup, picked up her discarded handbag and withdrew a long envelope. "She was also with Margaret when she died. That part of the story she wrote down for you. There was no doubt in her mind how desperately you were wanted and loved by your mother."

Hilda looked from one to the other, and then reverently reached out and took the letter. "I don't know if I can take much more just now," she muttered unsteadily. "I'll read this some other time."

"Good," said Rance fervently. Her eyes flew to his, and he gave her a twisted smile. "I mean, there are other things we need. . .I need to talk about."

Before Hilda could begin to wonder what on earth he wanted—no, needed—to talk to her about, Jean stood up and straightened her shoulders. "Yes, of course," she said with some of her old crispness back in her voice. "You have a lot of decisions to make, and I know we promised Nathan we wouldn't be too long before we went back to bring him to see Hilda."

They all heard the sound of a motor, and Rance suddenly scowled. "That sounds like he's already driven the Stevenses around the twist, and they couldn't wait to get rid of him!"

Hilda sprang to her feet with excitement. She was at the driveway before the car had rolled to a stop. It felt so wonderful to see Nathan's radiant face as he tumbled out of the car and into her arms.

Jim's face beamed widely at her over Nathan's head. He gave her the thumbs up sign and then waved as he put the car in motion again. She stared at him in some surprise, and then returned her attention to Nathan as he wriggled out of her hug.

His suddenly scowling face looked so incredibly like his father's a few moments before that she laughed in sheer delight and hugged him again. This time he pushed her away.

"Hildie, I missed you! Why'd you go away for so long!" he accused her.

"Well, just look at you, Nathan Telford! Don't you look great!" Hilda stared at him with delight. She was sure he had shot up. His thin body had filled out. His eyes were clear and sparkling with health and the delight of seeing her again.

"Son, I thought I told you we'd come for you when we were ready," Rance said with so much resigned annoyance that Nathan looked taken back.

"But you've been here for ages, Dad! You've had plenty of time to ask her—"

"Nathan!" roared Rance. "Not another word!"

"But, Dad, I only—"

Jean suddenly grabbed the small boy by the arm. "Nathan, we had other important things to talk about first, and your father hasn't had a chance, so not another word," she said ferociously.

"And if you didn't eavesdrop on other people's conversations, you wouldn't have known anything about it," Rance said through gritted teeth.

"I didn't eavesdrop!" Nathan declared vehemently. "A bloke can't help hearin' you two talkin' right outside his own room, can he? And anyway, it was a brilliant idea, just brilliant!" He turned to Hilda, and stopped abruptly. Surprise and then affront flashed across his face. "What are you laughin' at?"

Hilda had dissolved into delighted giggles. "You're talking at each other just like a perfectly normal father and son!"

Color crept into Rance's cheeks. "Yeah, I guess we are," he said sheepishly, "but I don't know why you find it so funny!"

"Oh, my dears, not funny, just such a relief!" Hilda beamed from one puzzled face to the other.

Nathan's mouth opened, but Jean spoke rapidly first. "Well, whatever Hilda and your dad are talking about, it must be okay, Nathan. Hilda, I do take it we can all stay the night?"

"Oh, can you stay? That would be marvelous!" Hilda was thrilled, and then suddenly she remembered. Her face stilled. "But won't Maree be expecting you?"

Utter astonishment flooded Rance's face, and Nathan asked with surprise, "Maree who?"

"Ah, that explains it!" Jean explained.

Hilda looked from one to the other with bewilderment.

Nathan didn't even know who Maree was? Could that possibly mean Rance had not told him yet? She opened her mouth, and then closed it with a snap as she saw the sudden challenge in Rance's eyes, and a flickering fire that looked like. . .looked like anger! Then he spoke, and she knew she was right. He was furious.

"Maree! Why that—" Rance snarled. Nathan jerked around and gaped at him, and he checked himself with an obvious effort. "We're long overdue for a long talk, it seems, Hilda Garrett! I'll get our stuff out of the car," he added in that same controlled voice that was even more frightening to Hilda. He started toward his car. "You come and help me, Nathan," he snapped over his rigid shoulders.

"Aunt Jean, what on earth's the matter with you all?" Hilda gasped as they disappeared.

Jean took her arm, and headed for the house. "Things have been in a muddle, that's for sure, but it's obvious to me there's absolutely nothing the matter," she said with an air of complete satisfaction that only further bewildered Hilda. Then Jean squeezed her arm gently and said tenderly, if a little shakily, "Or there won't be once you and Rance can get a chance to sort things out."

The normally efficient Hilda was all fingers and thumbs as she allocated bedrooms, organized linen, and left them to refresh themselves while she escaped to the kitchen. She grabbed some meat from the freezer to thaw in the microwave.

Then she suddenly sat down on a kitchen chair with trembling legs. It was beginning to all seem like a dream. Jean was her aunt. Rance had kissed her as though he had been as starved for her as she had been for him all these long weeks and months.

A low roll of thunder reverberated in the distance. Hilda

wiped a hand across her forehead. It was still very hot, even though it was quite dark now. Suddenly she felt stifled and made for the door.

Rain had been forecast several times the past couple weeks. The farmers in the area had been anxiously watching as heavy clouds had scurried across the sky many times without pausing to water their crops. Hilda had heard of heavy falls in some places, and had prayed that they would not miss out again. A good rain now would fill the heads of the wheat nicely.

Normally this part of the Downs enjoyed a dryer heat than those sweltering on the coast. Tonight, even when Hilda had slipped out of the house by the front door, the air was heavy and very humid.

Funny how hardly anyone ever came to the front door, she mused absently, trying to keep her thoughts off her unexpected guests. Sometimes strangers from the city, like machinery or insurance salesmen, knocked on the front door, but everyone else automatically drove up to the side gate and found their way to the back door. It was always the welcoming farm kitchen they made for.

Hilda had snatched up a torch on the way out, and shone it carefully in front of her as she walked. This burst of hot weather brought the snakes out from their winter inactivity, and she had learned to be very careful.

As she moved slowly away from the house and its surrounding trees, the great pillars of clouds in the east drew her attention. As she watched, distant jagged shafts of light illuminated them. At first they were too far away to hear anything, and then an occasional distant growl of thunder began to rumble.

The air was very still. Not a breath stirred the damp curls on her forehead. Between watching where she placed her feet and being entranced by the distant aerial display, she did not realize she had wandered so far from the house, until she paused and looked back the way she had come. One single beam of light escaped through the branches of the few fruit trees near the house.

Hilda felt tears pricking her eyes. This was her home, not that narrow, unpleasant Paddington street, but these wide open spaces. She had lived here with a pair of the finest people who could have become her parents. But what did the future hold for her now?

"Oh, Lord, I don't know how to thank You for everything You've done in my life," she prayed out loud. She gave a laugh of sudden joy and delight. It was drowned out by a loud crash of thunder that made her jump. "Oh, what can I do for You in return?" she cried loudly, "I need to show You how very much I love You and praise You!"

Another peel of thunder brought her eyes back to the storm. It was much closer now. A bolt of lightning lit up the sky. Thunder rumbled from horizon to horizon. Hilda had always loved storms. While her mother had cowered away inside, she would stand and watch in awe as the thunderbolts hurtled earthward across the flat plains.

Out here there was nothing between her and the angry sky. It was awesome, but it was getting too close. She turned to make her way back to the house. The next flash of light showed a dark shape moving toward her along the track.

"Hildie?"

Rance's voice. Calling out after the roll of thunder had died away.

"Coming, Rance" she called back.

Anytime, Rance. Just call, and I'll come.

She stumbled quickly along the track toward him. When she reached him, his hands went out and engulfed hers.

They stared at each other for a moment, and then she was being held close to him, and suddenly she knew that this was her home from now on. In the shelter of this wonderful man's arms. Oh, if only he felt the same way!

They stood that way for a long time. Suddenly there was a particularly brilliant flash of light and then another. They both turned instinctively toward the east as thunder rumbled around them.

"Aren't you afraid of storms?" Rance asked softly in the brief silence that followed.

"I love them!"

She found herself almost shouting as noise rose around them again. Exhilaration was rising in her. She felt herself beginning to tremble as his hand moved to cup her shoulders. He must have felt a tremor, and his fingers tightened their grip as a brilliant flash zigzagged across the sky and plunged into the earth. They tensed. Waited for the roar and crackle that followed.

"I've never seen anything like this," Rance said with awe.

"We get some truly magnificent storms sweeping across the flat plains." Hilda paused for another roll of thunder. "It's still quite a way off. It could be what we call a dry storm—little or no rain. We get a few of them usually much later every summer. Sometimes they start fires."

Hilda never knew how long they silently stood, as one, absorbed by the awesome display of power. The noise of the thunder kept getting closer. The time between the flashes and the thunder lessened. At last the air around them was filled with a never ending crackle and roar and crash.

"It's absolutely fantastic!" Hilda found herself trying to shout above the noise. A faint breeze sprang up, stirring the air around them. She was vaguely aware that Rance's arms were holding her tightly pressed against the front of him.

"Just a glimpse of God's almighty power!" his voice roared back exultantly.

They stood watching for several more spell binding minutes. A sheet of lightning ripped into the ground a little too close, even for Hilda. She shrank closer to the security and haven of the strong body behind her as the almost simultaneous thunder roared.

Rance's arms tightened. Hilda felt him tremble. She tensed. They turned and faced each other. One strong finger barely touched her cheek. It moved to her lips, and lingered there. Hilda knew she would not be able to bear it if he didn't hurry up and kiss her again. She moved closer. He stiffened, and then she felt the air expelled slowly from his lungs as he bent his head. This kiss was more tender, more full of love than Hilda had ever dreamed a kiss could be.

"Oh, Hildie, there's never been another woman like you." Rance's voice sounded hoarse, filled with awe and wonder. "I've missed you unbelievably these long weeks."

She only just heard him above the cacophony of noise. A couple of large drops of rain fell on them. He let her go and grabbed her hand.

"We'd better get under shelter as quickly as we can. This is no dry storm," he yelled above the now almost continuous clamour.

Suddenly they were laughing joyously, deliriously at each other. They ran as fast as they could over the rough track.

They were almost at the house when Rance yelled in her ear, "Anywhere we can talk besides the house?"

She nodded silently, and led him toward the shed a short distance past the house where the cars were garaged. Just as they arrived, one more ferocious roar of thunder announced the arrival of pelting rain. The impact of the rain was deafening on the corrugated roof, and Hilda gestured silently toward her car. Rance shook his head, and pulled her back into his arms against his full length and turned her so they could watch the rain.

She thought she heard him say faintly above the dreadful din, "I love it like this."

As she allowed him to mould his body to hers, her tumult of emotions slowly began to subside, even as the storm outside began to ease. Confusion swamped her, but there was one thing she was sure of now.

The storm died away, and still they held each other silently, until Hilda stirred and put her knowledge into words. "You aren't going to marry Maree." It wasn't a question, but a statement full of delighted wonder.

Rance changed his grip on her, and swung her around to face him. He took a deep breath, and said wonderingly, "Jean was right. You did think Maree and I had patched things up."

She nodded silently. Suddenly she pulled away from him and went over to a light switch. They both blinked in the sudden bright light, and then looked at each other.

"Did Maree say we had?" Anger flickered in Rance's dark eyes.

Hilda hesitated, thinking back. Suddenly she gave a rueful smile, "Probably she didn't really imply as much as I did to Gail about Jim." She pulled a face. "She was so absolutely confident, I didn't even question it. She said she'd arrived, and I'd lost. Your excitement the next morning seemed a confirmation."

"My excitement. . .?" Rance began with a puzzled frown as he thought back. Then his expression cleared. "Oh, I thought she'd told you that her father told her the church in Toowoomba was sending me a letter of apology and wanted me to resume the ministry there. I was really pleased because a lot of the folk had been very upset, and I knew this would begin the healing process for the church."

Then he scowled as he remembered what else Hilda had said. "As for that win and lose rubbish. . .she didn't have any say in the matter!" Rance said irritably. "I suppose you think she broke off our engagement because of Nathan like everybody else does."

Hilda's obvious astonishment gave him his answer.

"I was a fool," Rance said bluntly. "Last year, I felt pretty lonely. All my old student mates were happily married. I envied David his Kim and Jodie so much. Suddenly Maree was there." He gave an angry shrug. "She was beautiful. Never missed services or the mid-week Bible study I took. We talked at length about spiritual things. She seemed perfect for a minister's wife. Once again I ran ahead of the Lord, and let my heart rule my head."

"But even Dad thought she had broken it off because of Nathan," Hilda said in a dazed voice. Suddenly she wished Rance wasn't so far away. Even the short distance between them was unbearable.

"It all happened almost at the same time unfortunately," Rance said savagely. "It was very convenient for her to act the heart-broken, bewildered little woman. I found out that Maree had discovered I had a very rich step-father who had no children of his own. She'd worked out in her devious little mind that she could bear to be a minister's wife for a few years, and then she was sure when I inherited all his lovely money and properties, I'd be forced to leave the ministry to carry it all on for him."

Hilda felt a sudden shaft of unexpected sympathy for Maree. "That was a very logical conclusion for someone like Maree who only thought of your work in human terms," she said gently. "Only someone who really walks in the Spirit could understand your love for Jesus and realize your calling by Him to the ministry leaves you no choice."

Rance's eyes came alive again with love. "But you understand, Hildie darling, don't you? You'd always understand the words of the apostle Paul you quoted to me once before." He took a couple paces forward, and placed both of his large hands tenderly on each side of her flushed face. "Woe to me if I don't preach the Gospel," he whispered softly. A light kiss landed on her nose. "You understand, don't you?" he persisted. "I realized at that service centre at the freeway that we shared a spiritual oneness I never had with Maree."

She stood helplessly in his hands and simply stared at him.

"You would be there to help the Lord keep that minister on the right track, wouldn't you? You'd be his true right hand, his best friend, the mother of his children, his life's companion, and his wonderful lover," he whispered as his lips touched hers. "Oh, I do love you so much, sweetheart."

And then lips were clinging again, and there was only the taste of him, the feel of him, his strength, their mutual love, and increasing passion.

Hilda didn't know how long they kissed and murmured of their love, saying all the beautiful, foolish things lovers have said since time began, the hows, the whys, when each had recognized that love for the first time.

"It was that madam Jodie that clinched it for me," Rance chuckled softly. "A few seconds after she saw you, she asked me if you were the pretty lady who would be my Mummy!"

Right back then! When she was so worried about him.

He suddenly sighed, and loosened his tight hold on her. "I suppose we'd better get back to the house. It was such a relief when Jean told me she saw you heading off down the track. I was beginning to wonder if I'd ever get you away from Nathan."

He kissed her lightly on the lips, and then he groaned, and gathered her close again. Hilda willingly pressed against his body, giving him all he asked of her sweetness and love.

At last he gave a stifled groan, and lifted his head. "I suppose there'll be time later to make plans, but. . ." He hesitated and then said slowly, "You won't mind living in Brisbane for at least a few years will you, sweetheart?"

Hilda was still trying to come down from the heights, and said in a dazed voice, "Brisbane. Why would I be thinking of living in Brisbane?"

Sudden alarm flashed across Rance's face. "You. . .you'd rather I took the offer of the Toowoomba church?" He continued slowly, as he stared at her. "I suppose you don't want to live in a city, do you?"

Hilda gave her head a little shake, as much to clear it as to deny what Rance had just said. "I lived in Brisbane for a couple years when I was at university. It wasn't too bad. But why. . .?" Hilda's eyes opened wide as she suddenly realized what he was talking about. A thrill of delight and love swept through her.

For a moment she was speechless, and then her eyes began to dance mischievously. "Are you asking me to live with you, Reverend Rance Telford!" Her voice held mock alarm and horror.

He frowned. "Of course we'll—" He suddenly recognized the twinkle in her eyes, and her rapidly failing effort to keep from bursting into laughter. And then it dawned on him!

A few moments later, peel after peel of a radiant woman's laughter rang out from that old battered tin shed lit by a naked light bulb.

"For heaven's sake, woman!" grumbled Rance. "I thought this was the most serious question a bloke ever asked a woman. Now, will you be quiet and listen. It's horribly uncomfortable down—"

"Dad!" exclaimed an indignant voice. "Haven't you asked her yet?" Nathan stepped into the light. "What are you doing down there in the dirt?"

Rance glanced with horror over his shoulder and then jumped very self-consciously and quickly from his knees to his feet in one lithe movement. Hilda had just managed to stifle her giggles, but this set her off again. A moment later Rance's hearty roar joined her. They moved together and leaned helplessly against each other.

Nathan looked at them in disgust. He scuffed his heavily mud-coated sneaker, and scowled. "Well! Are ya' or aren't ya'?" he asked Hilda belligerently.

Rance managed to control his mirth enough to say, "There are better ways to propose, Nathan Telford!"

"And when you find one, you'd better show your father!" laughed Hilda.

Then her laughter faded away, and her face was radiant with love and tenderness as she glanced from the tall, fair man to his smaller replica. "And, it doesn't really matter a bit, after all." She gave a mock frown at Rance, and added quickly, "As long, of course, as there is no misunderstanding. If the question is, 'Will I marry you, and love you both for ever and ever?' the answer just has to be in the affirmative."

Nathan's frown was back. "Does that a. . .affirm business mean yes?" he asked anxiously.

Hilda let go of Rance, and crouched down to Nathan's level. "It sure does mean yes! You'd better believe it!" she said quite firmly.

The boy's face lit up. "Fantastic!" Then he suddenly turned on his heel and raced away. They heard his voice yelling, "Aunt Jean! She said yes! I've got a new Mum!"

Rance moved forward. He stretched out his hands. She reached up and clasped them, and he hauled her to her feet and into his arms again. She went, laughing and filled with love.

"Oh, well," Rance sighed, "I suppose that's just a taste of what it's going to be like down through the years when we try and sneak a few moments to ourselves away from the children."

"The children," Hilda said dreamily, and sighed with contentment at all that conjured up.

"And at least one dog, I suppose," added Rance glumly.

"A dog!"

Rance ran a gentle finger over her open mouth. "Of course. Little boys as well as little girls need a dog. Especially collie dogs called Polly," he said tenderly.

To his surprise, she shook her head wistfully. "No, not another Polly. There could only be one of her. Perhaps a Trixie, instead?"

He kissed her very tenderly. "Anything you say, my darling Hildie. Oh! I forgot!" Rance straightened. He looked down at her lovingly. "By the way, I meant to warn you. Don't let on to your Aunt Jean how much you've always hated 'Hilda' for a name."

The complete change of subject from dreams to such a mundane thing bewildered her. "Why ever not?" she asked sharply.

"I'm sorry, sweetheart," he answered her solemnly. "She told me very proudly once that Hilda has been at least one of the names for the first girl in your family for generations. Hilda was a chief goddess in German mythology. The name means 'battle' in Old German. It's Aunt Jean's second name, too!"

"Truly!" Delight flashed into Hilda's face, and then she scowled fiercely. "I'm sorry, too! Any poor girl we have will never be saddled with the wretched name, especially if it was the name of a goddess! And I've had enough battles to last several lifetimes. It's about time traditions like that from yesterday were well and truly forgotten!"

Much to Jean's disgust and Rance's bemusement, one day in the future, Hilda had her way.

She smiled radiantly down at the squawking little bundle in her arms, and said lovingly, "Hello, Margaret Jean Telford."

A much taller Nathan beamed at them both. "Hiya', Meg!" He held up a firmly held, squirming bundle of brown and white puppy, and added, "Meg, this is our dog, Trixie."

Meg? Hilda looked at him reproachfully, and then up at the proud, beaming Rance. He began to chuckle softly, and spread his hands out helplessly.

Hilda looked lovingly. . .mistily at him. Then her gaze was drawn down at the yawning infant. Her search for yesterday had not been wasted for a moment. God had shown her His overwhelming love and care in the past, and her heart knew beyond a shadow of doubt, there was even more of that never failing love to be revealed in the days still to come.

A Letter To Our Readers

Dear Reader:

In order that we might better contribute to your reading enjoyment, we would appreciate your taking a few minutes to respond to the following questions. When completed, please return to the following:

Rebecca Germany, Editor
Heartsong Presents
P.O. Box 719
Uhrichsville, Ohio 44683

1. Did you enjoy reading *Search for Yesterday*?
   ❑ Very much. I would like to see more books
   by this author!
   ❑ Moderately
   I would have enjoyed it more if _____

   _____

2. Are you a member of *Heartsong Presents*? Yes   No
   If no, where did you purchase this book? _____

   _____

3. What influenced your decision to purchase this
   book? (Check those that apply.)

   ❑ Cover   ❑ Back cover copy

   ❑ Title   ❑ Friends

   ❑ Publicity   ❑ Other _____

4. On a scale from 1 (poor) to 10 (superior), please rate the following elements.

    ___Heroine   ___Plot

    ___Hero   ___Inspirational theme

    ___Setting   ___Secondary characters

5. What settings would you like to see covered in *Heartsong Presents* books?

_____

_____

6. What are some inspirational themes you would like to see treated in future books?_____

_____

_____

7. Would you be interested in reading other *Heartsong Presents* titles? ❏ Yes ❏ No

8. Please check your age range:
❏ Under 18 ❏ 18-24 ❏ 25-34
❏ 35-45 ❏ 46-55 ❏ Over 55

9. How many hours per week do you read? —————

Name _____

Occupation _____

Address _____

City _____ State _____ Zip _____

Susannah Hayden

❀❀❀❀❀❀❀❀❀❀❀❀❀❀❀❀❀❀❀❀❀❀❀❀❀❀❀❀❀❀

__*A Matter of Choice*—Stacie's new job promotion could mean the end of her future with Brad. . .or the start of a new and perhaps better life with Dillon. What life is Stacie to have? HP14

__*Between Love and Loyalty*—Megan Browning and her friends are working frantically to keep the old Homestead Youth Camp running. Then Megan discovers that the young architect who has captured her heart is planning on developing Homestead into condominiums. HP69

__*The Road Before Me*—Overwhelmed by self-doubt, Julie Covington searches for an answer. At her grandmother's childhood home in Maine she finds comfort and solace in the writings of a young girl, a girl who walked the same road as the one before Julie. HP77

__*Between the Memory and the Moment*—Jenna seems happy living and working at the camp owned by Dillon Graves. After all, she's hopelessly in love with the much-older Dillon, and he genuinely appreciates her work. Still, Jenna feels compelled to move on. But to what? HP113

__*Farther Along the Road*—Julie Covington wants to be accepted as a serious artist, and she wants to possess a love as vital as the one her grandmother had for her first love. When Larry Paxton displays interest in her paintings, Julie begins to feel hopeful that both needs can be fulfilled. HP117

Send to: Heartsong Presents Reader's Service
P.O. Box 719
Uhrichsville, Ohio 44683

Please send me the items checked above. I am enclosing **$2.95** for *each* title, totaling $_____(please add $1.00 to cover postage and handling per order. OH add 6.25% tax. NJ add 6% tax.).

Send check or money order, no cash or C.O.D.s, please.

To place a credit card order, call 1-800-847-8270.

NAME _____

ADDRESS _____

CITY/STATE _____ ZIP _____

HAYDEN

Hearts♥ng

Any 12 *Heartsong Presents* titles for only $26.95 *

CONTEMPORARY ROMANCE IS CHEAPER BY THE DOZEN!

Buy any assortment of twelve *Heartsong Presents* titles and save 25% off of the already discounted price of $2.95 each!

*plus $1.00 shipping and handling per order and sales tax where applicable.

HEARTSONG PRESENTS TITLES AVAILABLE NOW:

_HP 3 RESTORE THE JOY, *Sara Mitchell*
_HP 4 REFLECTIONS OF THE HEART, *Sally Laity**
_HP 5 THIS TREMBLING CUP, *Marlene Chase*
_HP 6 THE OTHER SIDE OF SILENCE, *Marlene Chase*
_HP 9 HEARTSTRINGS, *Irene B. Brand**
_HP 10 SONG OF LAUGHTER, *Lauraine Snelling**
_HP 13 PASSAGE OF THE HEART, *Kjersti Hoff Baez*
_HP 14 A MATTER OF CHOICE, *Susannah Hayden*
_HP 18 LLAMA LADY, *VeraLee Wiggins**
_HP 19 ESCORT HOMEWARD, *Eileen M. Berger**
_HP 21 GENTLE PERSUASION, *Veda Boyd Jones*
_HP 22 INDY GIRL, *Brenda Bancroft*
_HP 25 REBAR, *Mary Carpenter Reid*
_HP 26 MOUNTAIN HOUSE, *Mary Louise Colln*
_HP 29 FROM THE HEART, *Sara Mitchell*
_HP 30 A LOVE MEANT TO BE, *Brenda Bancroft*
_HP 33 SWEET SHELTER, *VeraLee Wiggins*
_HP 34 UNDER A TEXAS SKY, *Veda Boyd Jones*
_HP 37 DRUMS OF SHELOMOH, *Yvonne Lehman*
_HP 38 A PLACE TO CALL HOME, *Eileen M. Berger*
_HP 41 FIELDS OF SWEET CONTENT, *Norma Jean Lutz*
_HP 42 SEARCH FOR TOMORROW, *Mary Hawkins*
_HP 45 DESIGN FOR LOVE, *Janet Gortsema*
_HP 46 THE GOVERNOR'S DAUGHTER, *Veda Boyd Jones*
_HP 49 YESTERDAY'S TOMORROWS, *Linda Herring*
_HP 50 DANCE IN THE DISTANCE, *Kjersti Hoff Baez*
_HP 53 MIDNIGHT MUSIC, *Janelle Burnham*
_HP 54 HOME TO HER HEART, *Lena Nelson Dooley*
_HP 57 LOVE'S SILKEN MELODY, *Norma Jean Lutz*
_HP 58 FREE TO LOVE, *Doris English*
_HP 61 PICTURE PERFECT, *Susan Kirby*
_HP 62 A REAL AND PRECIOUS THING, *Brenda Bancroft*
_HP 65 ANGEL FACE, *Frances Carfi Matranga*
_HP 66 AUTUMN LOVE, *Ann Bell*
_HP 69 BETWEEN LOVE AND LOYALTY, *Susannah Hayden*
_HP 70 A NEW SONG, *Kathleen Yapp*
_HP 73 MIDSUMMER'S DREAM, *Rena Eastman*

*Temporarily out of stock.

(If ordering from this page, please remember to include it with the order form.)

······· Presents ·······

*Temporarily out of stock.

Great Inspirational Romance at a Great Price!

Heartsong Presents books are inspirational romances in contemporary and historical settings, designed to give you an enjoyable, spirit-lifting reading experience. You can choose from 132 wonderfully written titles from some of today's best authors like Colleen L. Reece, Brenda Bancroft, Janelle Jamison, and many others.

When ordering quantities less than twelve, above titles are $2.95 each.

SEND TO: Heartsong Presents Reader's Service
P.O. Box 719, Uhrichsville, Ohio 44683

Please send me the items checked above. I am enclosing $ _____
(please add $1.00 to cover postage per order. OH add 6.25% tax. NJ add 6%.). Send check or money order, no cash or C.O.D.s, please.
To place a credit card order, call 1-800-847-8270.

NAME _____

ADDRESS _____

CITY/STATE_____ ZIP _____

HPS JULY

Hearts♥ng Presents
Love Stories Are Rated G!

That's for godly, gratifying, and of course, great! If you love a thrilling love story, but don't appreciate the sordidness of popular paperback romances, **Heartsong Presents** is for you. In fact, **Heartsong Presents** is the *only inspirational romance book club*, the only one featuring love stories where Christian faith is the primary ingredient in a marriage relationship.

Sign up today to receive your first set of four, never before published Christian romances. Send no money now; you will receive a bill with the first shipment. You may cancel at any time without obligation, and if you aren't completely satisfied with any selection, you may return the books for an immediate refund!

Imagine. . .four new romances every month—two historical, two contemporary—with men and women like you who long to meet the one God has chosen as the love of their lives. . .all for the low price of $9.97 postpaid.

To join, simply complete the coupon below and mail to the address provided. **Heartsong Presents** romances are rated G for another reason: They'll arrive *Godspeed!*